SPACEPOP

NOT YOUR AVERAGE PRINCESSES

[Imprint]
MAKE YOUR MARK

A part of Macmillan Children's Publishing Group

SPACEPOP: NOT YOUR AVERAGE PRINCESSES. Copyright © 2016 by Genius Brands.
International, Inc. All rights reserved.
Printed in the United States of America by R. R. Donnelley & Sons Company,
Harrisonburg, Virginia.
For information, address Imprint, 175 Fifth Avenue, New York, N.Y. 10010.

Library of Congress Cataloging-in-Publication Data is available.

ISBN 978-1-250-10227-0 (hardcover) / ISBN 978-1-250-10230-0 (ebook)

Our books may be purchased in bulk for promotional, educational, or business
use. Please contact your local bookseller or the Macmillan Corporate
and Premium Sales Department at (800) 221-7945 ext. 5442 or by
e-mail at MacmillanSpecialMarkets@macmillan.com.

Book design by Natalie C. Sousa
Imprint logo designed by Amanda Spielman
Illustrated by Jen Bartel

First Edition—2016

10 9 8 7 6 5 4 3 2 1

mackids.com

If you long for a life without gloom,
and wish to avoid Geela's Dungeon of Dark Doom,
leave this book in its rightful owner's room,
or you, naughty thief, will take it to your tomb.

SPACEP♥P

NOT YOUR AVERAGE PRINCESSES

ERIN DOWNING

[Imprint]
MAKE YOUR MARK

NEW YORK

SPECIAL THANKS to Erin Stein, rock star editor and collaborator (Sonny to my Cher, Simon to my Garfunkel, Donny to my Marie, Keith to my Mick, Hall to my Oates . . .), and to Michael Bourret, our very own Chamberlin

A SPECIAL ANNOUNCEMENT FROM EMPRESS GEELA:

This greeting is for all citizens living, working, and whining on the planets of the Pentangle: I am GEELA, and as of this moment I declare myself your new EMPRESS!

Henceforth, the planets of the Pentangle— Lunaria, Junoia, Rhealo, Heralda, and Athenia—will be under my control. The glorious, magnificent, and most adored Dark Empress of Evil has taken over.

Any questions or complaints should be directed to a member of my faithful Android army, who would be happy to find a new home for you in the DUNGEON OF DARK DOOM.

"And . . . *cut!*" Geela—the self-appointed Dark Empress of Evil—smirked as she finished recording her special announcement for the galaxy. "That should get the message across." She turned to a guard and ordered, "Play that for the people of the Pentangle after we rid them of their filthy royalty!"

With a casual flick of her wrist, Geela dismissed her Android army. "Now, go! Go forth and take the royal families of the Pentangle prisoner. It is *my* turn to rule the Galaxy!" The imposing metallic troops scattered quickly. No one who worked for the evil empress ever wanted to be left alone with her. Geela had a creepy habit of melting creatures with her eyes when she was in a bad mood. She had also been known to wrap her tongue around her victims' necks and squeeze them to death. Her razor-sharp fingernails could shoot out at 452 miles per hour to stop an enemy dead in his tracks. In short, she was not the kind of lady anyone wanted to mess with . . . not even heavily armed guards.

Geela stroked her small, winged sidekick. "Ah, Tibbitt," she crooned, her face morphing into a gruesome smile. Tibbitt stood dutifully by her side. The dragon-like creature—with a disturbingly humanlike head—had been in Geela's service for years. The empress's late father passed him down to Geela, and during his years with the family, Tibbitt had become an expert listener and sounding board. "The time has finally come for my complete takeover of the Pentangle Galaxy."

Tibbitt sighed happily in response.

"As soon as I've had my coffee and a doughnut," she crooned. "I will attack each of the five revolting planets of the Pentangle, rule their people myself with a long magnificent reign as empress, and—just to make sure no one bothers me—I'll lock the royal families in . . ." Geela paused dramatically, lifted her arms into the air and screamed, ". . . the Dungeon of Dark Doom on Sector Nine!"

She tipped back her head and laughed—a horrible, honking sound that almost made Tibbitt flinch. Geela sneered, "Oh yes, that's right. All five of the ridiculous royal families are going down. The time for 'getting along' and 'living in peace' is *over*. Royalty-schmoyalty!"

Beside her, Tibbitt carefully matched his expression to Geela's and snickered.

The empress switched over to a nasal, whining voice and went on. "All these silly princesses and kings and queens, who think they're *so special* just because they were *born royal*. Ha!" She shook her fist in the air. "Royal blood doesn't make you more deserving, more beautiful, or more loved. I'll prove to all of them that I am a better ruler than any of them, even though I have *no* royal blood running through my ice-cold veins. Let's show the planets of the Pentangle who their *new* ruler is."

Tibbitt cocked his head curiously.

Geela violently twisted his ear and laughed her savage laugh. "I'm talking about *me*, you fool. After today, the new leader of the entire Pentangle Galaxy will be *meeeeeee!*"

PART ONE: *THE ESCAPE*

LUNA

THE PLANETS OF THE PENTANGLE WERE IN GRAVE danger, but Princess Lunaria de Longoria was still in bed. "Hello?" the princess called out in a soft, expectant voice. When there was no response, she raised her voice and hollered, "Hel-*lo*! Is *anyone* going to bring me my juice? It is now one full minute after nine."

There were no sounds from the hall outside her royal bedroom. That was odd. Usually, the palace was bustling with the *swish-swish* and *spritz-spritz* sounds of cleaning, or the quick patter of servants hustling to and fro, or her mother's firm voice barking out a list of daily tasks for the palace employees. But this morning, the halls of the Palace of Lunaria were still and strangely silent.

Princess Lunaria pushed back her smooth satin sheets and flexed her buttery-yellow feet. She inspected the elegant designs painted on each of her big toenails. She wasn't due to have her weekly pedicure for two days, but she wasn't sure she could stand to wait that long. A tiny fleck of polish had chipped off when she stepped out of the shower the previous morning, and she was growing tired of the color on her toes. It felt dated—very last week. She made a mental note to have someone call down to the palace spa later.

With a heavy sigh, the princess craned her neck and waited. She blinked her eyes—one a bright yellow, the other vibrant orange—impatiently. Usually, all it took was a simple call and *someone* would come running. She clanged the little bell she'd had installed by her bedside, then listened intently. Nothing. Frustrated, she opened her mouth and released a loud scream that spanned eight octaves. Her pampered and loving pet, Adora, snuggled deeper into the covers beside her, trying to catch a few more minutes of sleep. The cuddly pink and red creature groaned, irritated at having been disturbed. Then, with a soft sigh, Adora tucked all four of her delicate paws under her soft body and fell back to sleep.

A moment later, Lunaria heard an unfamiliar *thump-thump-thump* coming from somewhere far below her bedroom in one of the palace's great rooms. Out the window, a strange buzzing sound drowned out the usual birdsong in the gardens.

The princess pressed a button on her bed's headboard, and the sweet sound of her own singing floated out of the speakers that were hidden around the room. Much better.

After another quick peek at the time—*nine-oh-four*!— Lunaria flopped back onto a heavenly stack of pillows and growled. Where *was* everyone? Like a true princess, Lunaria de Longoria did not like to be kept waiting. And she usually refused to get out of bed in the morning until she had nourished her body with a tall glass of green juice pressed from the palace's garden vegetables. She set her mouth into a firm scowl, but relaxed the muscles into a soft pout when she caught a glimpse of her reflection in the mirror hanging over her bed. Scowling didn't suit her lovely features.

Lunaria dropped her legs over the side of her round, floating bed and landed gracefully on the plush carpet below. She wanted juice! It was highly unusual to do something for herself. She tiptoed to the door of her bedroom, cocked her head, and listened hopefully for the telltale sound of a servant's footsteps in the hallway. She smiled when she heard someone approaching her door. *About time*, she mused. She would have to give this servant a little talking to. A wait this long was totally unaccept-able. The door of her room flew open, and Lunaria jumped back.

"Excuse me," she snapped, glaring at the intruder. "I believe it is best to *knock* before entering a princess's quarters?"

The unfamiliar man standing in the doorway arched an eyebrow and bowed—but only slightly. "Apologies, Your Highness."

"That's better," Lunaria said stiffly, arching one of her own perfect eyebrows back at him. "And next time, I expect you to present yourself with a proper bow. That little curtsy, or whatever it was—weak."

She narrowed her eyes and studied the servant more carefully. The princess had never seen this guy before. He was old—really old. Display-in-a-museum old. Lunaria suddenly felt a little bad for picking on such a frail crea-ture. The man was breathing heavily, as if he'd run to her room in a hurry. As he should have—she had been wait-ing for her juice for *six minutes* already!—but the hustle had clearly winded the old guy. She hoped he wouldn't die from the effort. Juice was important, but probably not *that* important.

Studying the man more closely, Princess Lunaria had a sudden realization that the guy might not be *able* to bow. If he bent over, he might never be able to stand upright again. He'd just fold in half and stay that way for the rest of his life. Which probably wasn't much longer, to be honest.

"Or perhaps you *can't* bow?" Lunaria asked the servant, loudly and slowly. She wondered if he was so old he couldn't even hear anymore? It was actually quite generous of her parents to employ someone so ancient. It bothered her that *she* had to deal with the old geezer, but she was willing to do *some* charity work now and again. So she made her voice even louder and asked, "Does it hurt your old frail joints to bow?"

The man cleared his throat. "Your Highness," he said in a surprisingly commanding voice. "Your planet is in danger. Your people are in danger. *You* are in danger. We must get you out of here immediately."

"You, sir, are the one in danger," Lunaria scoffed. "In case you hadn't noticed: I. Haven't. Had. My. Juice."

There was an enormous crash somewhere in another wing of the palace. Adora gave a short yip of alarm. The old man stepped into Lunaria's room and closed the door quickly. "If you please," he said warmly, though there was a nervous edge to his voice. "I am Chamberlin, the senior butler in Athenia's royal court."

"You're Chamberlin," Lunaria echoed, putting one hand on her hip. She batted her golden eyes and said, "And *I* am waiting. For my juice."

Chamberlin heaved a sigh, then rustled around in a small spacepack that had been strapped to his stooped shoulders. With a grim smile, he pulled out a wrinkled silver drink pouch. He thrust it at the princess. "Drink up and let's go, Princess."

She stared at the container of orange liquid, horrified. "What *is* that?"

"Juice," the old man grumbled. "Sort of." With a subtle roll of his eyes, Chamberlin pulled a small straw off the back of the juice pack and pushed it into the pouch. He held it out in front of Lunaria's face again and said, "I always keep one of these with me in case of emergencies. Drink, Your Highness."

She reached forward, offered him a small, inauthentic smile, and took the juice. A moment later, she shrieked and shoved the pouch back into his hands. "It's cold!" she said. "I don't hold cold things. I need you to wrap it in a cozy. Or you must hold it for me. My hands are delicate."

Chamberlin closed his eyes as another crash rang out somewhere below them. He muttered, "I will *not* hold it for you. Unless your hands are broken, you can hold your own juice. My service to the galaxy is keeping you and four other princesses safe, not feeding you. I am your bodyguard and your guide. And *you* are not a baby."

Lunaria's mouth flew open. "How *dare* you speak to me in such a way! I'll have you fired."

"You will do no such thing," Chamberlin said curtly. "Your Highness, you and I will be spending quite a lot of time together whether you like it or not. I have been given the rather, uh . . . *unpleasant* . . . task of ushering you to safety. So-called Empress Geela is coming for you at any moment. As the senior butler in the Pentangle court, your parents have charged me with the task of getting you and the other four Princesses of the Pentangle somewhere safe."

Lunaria took a small sip of juice. Then her face dropped. For a moment, it seemed as if she felt somewhat bad for her stubborn attitude. But a second later she whispered, "I'm supposed to share a butler with four other princesses?"

Suddenly, thundering footsteps filled the hallway outside the princess's chamber. As Chamberlin peeked through the crack in the door, his face paled. He reached out and locked the door. "We must go. Now. All the servants are fleeing—if we don't go immediately, while there is a good amount of activity in the corridor, we will be noticed."

"Chambermaid . . ." Lunaria said, holding up a hand. "Or whatever you said your name is? Hold on a sec. I just need to pack."

"Pack?" Chamberlin coughed. "There isn't time. You could be captured."

"Captured?" Lunaria asked. "You are so *dramatic.*"

"Perhaps I haven't made myself clear: Your parents have already been taken prisoner. If we fail in our escape, Empress Geela will also take you—and me—prisoner." The butler looked around Princess Lunaria's room, taking in the lush decor, three walk-in closets filled with elegant fashion, and a small fortune worth of lotions, powders, and makeup. Thinking quickly, Chamberlin said, "If you are caught, you will be forced to wear a shapeless jumpsuit, fed grilled space sardines, and locked in a dry cell . . . without moisturizers or lipstick."

Lunaria choked back a sob as loud voices echoed in the front hall of the palace below. Chamberlin had finally gotten through to her.

Adora hopped off the bed, scampered over, and weaved in and out of Lunaria's legs. The princess picked her up and nuzzled her face into the soft fur. She whimpered, "Geela took my parents? She is here now?"

Chamberlin looked nervously toward the door, then nodded. "Now, Your Highness. I am sorry to deliver such difficult news."

"What should we do?" she asked, panicking.

The butler looked around Lunaria's chamber, searching for some way to hide the princess. His eyes finally settled on an enormous rolling laundry hamper tucked into the far corner of the room. "In here," he said, pushing the hamper toward the door. "Hop in here and hide beneath the dirty clothes."

The princess's eyes bulged. "Never."

Chamberlin gulped as someone pounded on the door. "You must."

"I won't!" The pounding got louder. Someone rattled the latch. Then the door began to shake and vibrate—someone was slicing through the lock on Lunaria's beautiful, hand-carved mahogany door with a laser cutter. The princess looked from the door to the laundry hamper, her eyes wild. Adora hopped into the hamper without a second thought. She was a creature that didn't handle danger (or dirt) well.

"Would you like one more sip of juice before we go?" Chamberlin offered generously.

Lunaria reached out and grabbed the juice pouch. Then, just as the door was blasted open, she launched herself into the hamper full of dirty linens. Chamberlin dropped the lid closed just as two of Geela's soldiers raced into the room.

"Have you seen the princess?" Lunaria heard one of them bark out as Chamberlin rolled her toward the door and safety.

"She is in the spa," Chamberlin said, his voice shaking

slightly. "Getting her nails done, I believe." Then he tipped the hamper, rolled it into the hall, and hustled toward the exit as fast as his creaky limbs would allow.

Inside the hamper, both Adora and Lunaria whined quietly as Chamberlin whisked them toward a waiting escape ship. What the precious princess and her pampered pet had yet to realize was this: hiding inside a basket of dirty linens was bad . . . but what was to come was much, much worse.

JUNO

ON THE OTHER SIDE OF THE PENTANGLE GALAXY, Princess Junoia Atley-Wolford was just finishing up her morning run along the cliff's edge when she sensed danger. Slowing to a jog, she tilted her head to one side, listening intently for unfamiliar sounds. There were low booming sounds coming from the other side of the forest—near the capitol. Junoia's pet and running companion, Skitter, stilled beside her and sniffed at the air.

Junoia listened, her ears picking out all the strange sounds. At the age of ten, Junoia had spent a month learning to survive—and thrive—in the barren outlands on her home planet. As was the custom on the planet

Junoia, the princess had been forced to earn her independence by living on her own with no supervision or support. During that time, she had developed excellent instincts and a fighter's strength. Now, at fifteen, those instincts often proved helpful. Later, her strength would be a true asset as well.

The booming continued. It was unfamiliar to hear such a mechanical sound in the forested landscape. "What is that, Skitter?" Junoia asked, narrowing her dark violet eyes.

Snort snort, Skitter replied. Then the purple fluff ball held its breath and began to grow. When shy Skitter felt threatened, the little critter could puff up to twenty times her usual size.

"Hold off, pal," Junoia cautioned her. She patted Skitter on the back. "We don't know what those sounds are, and I don't want you calling any unwanted attention our way."

Skitter stopped growing and released little *pfft-pfft* sounds from her backside. With each little puff of air, the critter began to shrink again.

Suddenly, a form stepped out of the swirling morning mist. It approached the princess and Skitter slowly, but with purpose. Princess Junoia's body tensed, ready for a fight.

There was something about the way the stranger

moved that told her to hold off from attacking. Although it was difficult, she kept herself from lunging at the stranger. She had a sense that whoever it was did not mean to harm her. She stepped toward the stranger cautiously, and a moment later the stooped figure called out, "Princess Junoia Atley-Wolford?"

"What's it to you?" the princess called back. Skitter snuffed at the dirt on the hillside, then began pawing at the ground like a miniature bull. She—like her master—was always ready for a fight.

"I'm here to lead you to safety," the man said, his voice just loud enough to reach her.

Junoia snorted. The guy—now she could see that the creature was male, and he appeared to be very old—looked capable of leading *no one* to safety. Leading someone to a tea party, maybe. But to safety? Not a chance. He looked so frail that Junoia was shocked he hadn't yet been blown away by the wind blasting along the cliff's edge. "*You* want to lead *me* to safety?" she asked. "Safety from what, exactly?"

"Empress Geela, Your Highness," the man told her. "My name is Chamberlin, and I am the senior butler on the planet of Athenia."

Junoia put her hands on her slim, athletic hips. "If you're a butler on Athenia, what in the name of Grock are you doing here on Junoia? I hate to break it to you, but a guy like you doesn't really belong up here on the cliffs. A rough gust could blow you away like space-grass."

"I will explain everything in time, Your Highness, but for now, allow me to lead you to safety. It is my solemn duty."

The princess tried not to laugh. "Okay, you do that."

She watched, amused, as Chamberlin scanned the rugged landscape of her beloved home planet. If he were hoping a lighted path would appear out of the mist to show him the way to safety, he was going to be sorely disappointed. Maybe that's the sort of thing that happened on other planets in her galaxy, but not here. On Junoia you had to make your own path. "I thought . . ." the butler muttered. "I thought I'd come from that way, but no . . . ah . . . where was that landing bay?"

Chamberlin rubbed his chin. Junoia choked back a laugh. She stuffed her hands in her pockets and cocked her head. "Lost, are you? Who's supposed to be saving whom here?"

Princess Junoia had heard just enough about the princesses on the *other* planets of the Pentangle to be certain that she was the least princess-like of them all. They were all probably made of nothing but big hair and fancy gowns and snobby voices—unlike her family, who were super laid back and knew how to laugh and have fun like regular people. And they could also save themselves. They didn't need a butler to hold their hands when the going got rough.

If she had sensed any threat at all from Chamberlin, Junoia wouldn't have hesitated to leave the old guy stranded in the mist. But the royal butler seemed like a decent enough fellow. And from what she could tell, he truly did seem to believe she was in some sort of danger. "C'mon," she said, waving him in the direction of the capitol. "Let me lead you back to the palace."

"No!" Chamberlin said in an urgent voice. "We mustn't return to your home. Empress Geela is waiting for you there. I promised your parents I would lead you to safety—away from Junoia. Beyond this galaxy, even."

Junoia narrowed her eyes at him. "My parents told you to take care of me? You must think I'm a fool. I've been capable of taking care of myself since I was ten. They would never ask a crusty old butler to feed me and wash my clothes."

"They did not ask me to do any of *those* things, miss," Chamberlin said curtly. "As the oldest servant in the royal court of the Pentangle, I have been entrusted with your life and the lives of four other princesses. This task is a sacred duty, and I have sworn to fulfill it at any cost."

The booming sounds started up again. The tiny hairs

on the back of Junoia's neck stood tall. "Geela is . . . the Empress?" she asked. "And she's here on my planet? Really?" The princess glared at him. But Chamberlin didn't need to say any more—she believed him. She could sense the danger. "I need to go back to help my family," she insisted. "All the palace staff . . . and my people."

"It's too late," Chamberlin said. "Your family is long gone. She took your parents, and they are now her prisoners. The servants have been dismissed. And the ordinary citizens of Junoia are not the ones she has come for—she can control them in other ways. Today, she's come for you. You must leave now, before she finds you. Or me."

Without another word, Princess Junoia jumped into action. She grabbed Chamberlin by the arm and raced along the cliff's edge. The wind blasted her from all sides, but Junoia didn't stop. Skitter kept pace beside them, and Chamberlin stumbled along as quickly as he could. Suddenly, Junoia came to an abrupt stop.

Chamberlin wiped his brow and took deep breaths to recover. But the princess paused for only a moment, then she scrambled off the edge of the cliff. Rocks broke off the rough wall, bumping and thumping down to the sea below. "This way," Junoia ordered, urging Chamberlin to follow her.

"Oh no," the elderly butler said firmly. He planted his feet on solid ground and refused to budge. "I don't do climbing. As the great author, uh, once said: 'Foolish is a man who steps on unsteady rock.'"

"Come on," Princess Junoia said. "That's not a real saying. You just made it up."

"Ah, but it *is* a real saying," Chamberlin argued. The drone of Android ships buzzed over the forest—Geela's army would reach them at any moment.

"Well, then, today you'll have to be foolish." Junoia grabbed Chamberlin's arm and pulled him over the edge of the cliff. He stumbled, grasping for a handhold. "Don't worry," she told him, smiling grimly. "We're not going all the way down to the sea. Just a few feet down, there's a tunnel that will lead us to the other side of the woods. We can skirt around Geela's troops and get out of here."

"Wonderful . . ." Chamberlin muttered. Climbing along a cliff's edge, then crawling through a tunnel? Chamberlin was beginning to realize his new job was filled with perks. He grunted and heaved himself into the seemingly endless tunnel, trying to keep up with the princess. Under his breath he sighed, "I am far too old for this nonsense."

RHEA

BEEP BEEP! THE SHRILL HORN OF A SPACE CAB echoed off the smooth stone wall surrounding Rhealo's royal palace. Several single-alien transports replied with beeps and honks of their own. Two spaceports nearly knocked into each other before spiraling off to opposite sides of the narrow space-traffic lane.

"Watch it, pal," Princess Rhealetta Hemmings said, gracefully sidestepping the slow-moving traffic. She pounded the door of a space cab that nearly knocked into her and shot the two-headed driver a look that could kill. The driver made a rude gesture, obviously unaware that he had almost wounded royalty. "What's your rush?"

she snapped, her blue eyes flashing. "The spaceway is totally jammed!"

Geela's Android army had really messed up traffic in the center of Rhealo's capitol. When the evil empress and her crew of awful henchmen arrived on the planet to take the king and queen prisoner, the aftermath of their visit had left SR-8 at a standstill. The only option for getting out of town was public transportation—the space bus and transit shuttle lanes were the only things moving.

When an old butler named Chamberlin had appeared in the princess's chambers less than an hour earlier to tell her she had to get out of town—and off her planet for a while—she hadn't believed him at first. She thought the servants in the palace were playing some sort of prank on her, sending this strange and stiff guy to freak her out. But after a few minutes of banter, she'd realized the old man was totally serious.

She'd listened intently as Chamberlin told her that the king and queen—who weren't her parents, but related by ancient blood—had already been captured, and she was next on Geela's hit list. The princess had to scoot, he said, and fast. Cloaked in a ratty old blue cape that was almost the exact color of her smooth skin, the princess had barely managed to hide her pet Springle and slip out a side door of the palace unnoticed just five minutes earlier. Now, she, Springle, and Chamberlin had to get off the planet before Geela caught up to them.

Since Chamberlin clearly didn't know his way around Rhealo, Princess Rhealetta had come up with the only escape plan she could think of. She was going to hijack a space bus, disguise herself as the driver, and blast out of town. It wasn't brilliant, but it was something.

"What about that one over there?" Rhealetta asked Chamberlin, pointing to a rusted space bus that had stalled in the public transport lane. The driver was fiddling with some wiring on the side of the vehicle, so the captain's pod was empty and open.

"I don't know that I approve of this plan," Chamberlin said, stalling. "I would prefer we take one of the palace's approved vehicles. It is paramount that I keep you safe, Princess."

"I don't know that we have a choice at the moment," Rhealetta said, smiling. "We need to get off the planet, right? Traffic is at a standstill in the single-vehicle lanes. So we can either sit here waiting for things to clear up—which would make it pretty easy for Geela to swoop in and grab us—or we can nab a bus, have some fun, and get out of here." Springle shivered and chirped to express her agreement.

"When you put it that way . . ." Chamberlin said, nervously.

"When I put it that way, you feel *great* about stealing a bus, yes?" Rhealetta tilted her head under the heavy blue cloak and grinned. Springle bounced along beside them, her pink and blue body bouncing through the traffic. "This is gonna be fun!"

Chamberlin shook his head. After spending the morning with Princesses Lunaria, Junoia, and now Rhealetta, he was fairly certain he had made a big mistake when he agreed to take on this mission. Ushering the princesses to safety was of great importance to their galaxy, of course, but he had expected the mission to be much more straightforward than it was proving to be.

Rhealetta dashed across four lanes of crawling traffic, hopping and skipping toward the stalled bus. Chamberlin stumbled along after her, muttering hasty apologies and yelping every time he came too close to floating cars or space pods.

Without pausing, the princess leaped into the cab of the space bus and pressed the start button. The rambling motor roared to life, and outside the bus the driver shouted a surprised, "*Oy!*"

Rhealetta stuck her arm out the transport's front window and waved. She called, "Looks like she's fixed. If you don't mind me taking her for a joy ride, I'd be grateful for the lift. The people of our planet—and I—will thank you for your service someday." Without waiting for an answer, Princess Rhealetta revved the engine.

Chamberlin leaped into the bus and fumbled around in his pocket for the right fare. "Chamberlin, my man," Rhealetta said as she put the bus in gear and blasted away from the palace, "put your money away. This ride is on me."

Chamberlin sunk into a plastic bus seat and closed his eyes. "Would you like me to drive, Your Highness?" he offered, already knowing what the answer would be.

"Not a chance," Rhealetta said, swerving to miss a shuttle that had slowed to collect passengers. "This beats gaming—big time." She raced the stolen bus down the public transport lane. But after they'd gone only a few blocks, the bus wheezed and slowed to a crawl. Rhealetta slammed her hand against the wheel, frowning. "It's broken."

Springle wildly punched at the control panel, knocking off buttons and knobs with each swipe of her paws. Rhealetta's pet loved to try to help—but usually just caused trouble when she got involved in the princess's projects.

"Not broken," Chamberlin said, peering over her shoulder at the control panel. "It looks like this bus is programmed to pick up passengers at regular intervals along the route. We have no choice but to stop and collect a few fares."

The bus slowed, then stopped. The door of the transit sighed open, and a line of impatient passengers flooded into the bus. One by one, they dropped tokens, cards, and credits into the payment console. None of the passengers looked at their driver closely enough to realize it was the princess in the captain's pod. Rhealetta held her hand over her mouth, hiding a laugh. She hadn't left the palace without being recognized for years! Hiding among the people of her planet was so exciting.

Behind her, Chamberlin drummed his fingers together, muttering, "Hurry up, hurry up."

Princess Rhealetta turned around and whispered, "Chill, Chamberlin. We'll get out of here eventually—safe and sound. You can trust me." She winked at him. "What's your rush, anyway? You got a free ride, so quit your moaning! If we have to escape, let's at least have some fun."

HERA

"OMMM . . . OMMMM . . ." PRINCESS HERAZANNA Appleby lifted her face to the setting sun, took in a cleansing breath, then let it back out. She stretched her slender, sun-kissed pink arms up to the sky, waving at a small blue butterfly that floated past. "Hello, little butterfly!" she chirped.

It had been a beautiful day. The princess loved nothing more than having the opportunity to express gratitude for happy days with meditation and yoga. Beside her, Herazanna's feisty pink pet—Roxie—made soft little chittering sounds as she rolled around and around merrily in the soft grass.

As soon as she had finished her yoga practice, the

princess ran through the fields that surrounded her family's palace, gathering up handfuls of daisies and sun buttons. She wove the white and red flowers together into a wreath and placed it atop her head. She would give it to her mom when she returned to the palace. The colors would look lovely in her golden hair. After making a tiny wreath for Roxie to wear, the princess blew handfuls of kisses toward the sky and skipped through the fields back toward home.

But before she could reach the palace gates, the landscape around her went black. Some sort of shadow blotted out the sun overhead. Herazanna scratched her head. Just moments ago, the sky had been clear. The usually pink sky of Heralda had been awash in golden-teal streaks as the sun set on the horizon. There were no clouds in sight.

The princess looked up at her family's beautiful castle, searching for her mother's familiar silhouette in the window of the library. She wasn't there. That was strange. Her mother spent most afternoons in the library, reading fairy tales and looking out over the orchards.

"Maybe she's making a pie!" Herazanna guessed. She hoped she was right. Her mother's pies were extraordinary. Shrugging off the strange and sudden darkness, the carefree princess hustled toward the castle. If she hurried, she might get to the kitchens in time to help sprinkle sugar and cinnamon over the crust! That was the best part.

But before she reached the castle's front gate, a hand reached out from under a willow tree and pulled the princess into the canopied space beneath the branches.

"Hello!" Herazanna said, smiling at the stranger. On the planet of Heralda, most people were friendly and trustworthy, and there was almost no reason to worry about strangers who approached. Herazanna had found that when you greeted people with kindness and an open heart, they usually responded in a similar fashion. Besides, Roxie had already sniffed around the stranger's ankles and deemed him safe (by delicately chewing and snipping at the bottom of the man's pants leg), so the princess felt totally at ease.

The older fellow nodded politely and introduced himself. "Princess Herazanna, my name is Chamberlin."

"It's lovely to meet you, Chamberlin!" Herazanna said, curtsying. "Are you here for pie?"

"Pie? Ah . . . no." Then the man called Chamberlin launched into an explanation of why he was visiting the princess's home planet. He had come to help her, he said. The evil Empress Geela was on Heralda, and she had horrible things planned.

At the beginning of Chamberlin's story, the princess smiled and nodded, but when he told her that her parents had been taken prisoner, her bright smile faded. He finished by saying, "Your parents—and the other royal families of the Pentangle—have entrusted me with your care. We must go now, or Geela will find you, too. She is here." He gestured to the sky. "That is her starship, blocking out the sun."

"I see," Herazanna said softly, through her tears. She looked up at the ship, only slightly surprised she hadn't noticed it before. "I trust you, Chamberlin. I have only one question: Can I return to the castle for some of my things? And to say goodbye to the staff?"

"I'm sorry," Chamberlin said kindly. "But there isn't time."

Herazanna nodded. "Shall we meditate before we go? It will help to clear our minds and prepare our bodies for the journey ahead."

Chamberlin shook his head. "We haven't time for that either. Our ship is waiting. We must make haste, or you and the other princesses will be in even greater danger."

The princess sighed. "Gotcha." She twirled a lock of her hair around her pinky finger, thinking. Suddenly, she was all business. "Okay, if we want to get away from the castle without being noticed, we'll need to go by water." She pointed to the edge of the orchard. "There is a stream at the edge of the fruit fields that will take us to the landing bay near Strawberry Vale. From there, we will be able to circle around to where your ship is waiting."

The princess gathered her skirt into her fists and set off at a run. Roxie tumbled along behind her, and Chamberlin struggled to keep up. When they reached the water's edge, Herazanna pulled a homemade stick raft out from under some bushes. She untied it and brought it to shore. "Hop on!" she told Chamberlin.

The butler looked at the raft suspiciously. It looked tippy, and he wondered how it could possibly keep both of them afloat. Vehicles like this one were very much against protocol on his home planet of Athenia.

"Come on, silly," Herazanna said with a laugh. "Or would you rather swim?"

Timidly, Chamberlin climbed onto the wooden raft. He sat gingerly in the center of the raft, trying to keep as still as possible so water wouldn't splash up over the edge onto his good pants.

But a moment later, Herazanna leaped onto the raft and sent a tidal wave of warm water up and over Chamberlin's head. He spluttered and wiped at his eyes, muttering disapproving comments under his breath.

The river's current was gentle, so the raft moved downstream slowly at first. But as they made their way out of the castle grounds, the little raft began to pick up speed. All sorts of water creatures popped up out of the water as they made their way along the meandering stream. "Hello, Octo!" Herazanna cried to an enormous finned beast. "Hi, Gene!" she said, wiggling her fingers at a whiskered, three-headed creature.

A small flock of water birds floated along beside them, chirping out a relaxing melody. Herazanna hummed along with the birds, trying to keep her mind off what was happening back home. Then she pulled out a lute and began to play a sad goodbye song for the creatures of her planet.

Despite the tense task at hand, Chamberlin yawned every few seconds. Heralda was a dreamy sort of place, and the day's excitement had begun to catch up with him. The raft rocked and swayed, and the princess played her music on and on. They were still a mile from their escape ship when Herazanna's guide and protector, Chamberlin, fell fast asleep. Some planets just do that to even the most reliable of fellows.

ATHENA

METTATHENA MYSTOS HAD WAITED AS LONG AS possible, but the moment had finally come for her to leave her planet, Athenia, and her people. For hours, she had stayed strong, helping to secure the royal grounds. She had made arrangements to ensure that everyone in the palace would have access to essential supplies while the royal family was absent. Mettathena wasn't the type of princess to linger in long and tender goodbyes, but she felt duty-bound to take care of the staff who had kept an eye on her for years. She had no idea how long she or her parents would be gone.

"Ready, Mykie?" Mettathena asked her teddy bear–like

pet, a highly intelligent critter that was also Mettathena's only real friend.

Mykie cheeped back.

The princess lifted Mykie into an elaborate baby carriage and tucked her under a pile of blankets. Mettathena secured a baby bonnet over her pet's head and grimaced. "There."

Mykie growled and ripped at the blankets, refusing to settle down.

Mettathena shushed her. "I know, I know," she muttered. "I hate wearing silly costumes as much as you do—it's very childish. But if we want to escape without being noticed, we must slip out of the palace in disguise. And that means you, my friend, are going to ride out of here in a baby carriage. So deal with it and play your part." Mykie whimpered like a baby, and Mettathena patted at her in the carriage. "That's better."

She pushed the baby carriage down the long hallways of the royal palace, remembering every few steps to coo and smile down at her "baby" in the carriage. Through the glass-walled corridors, she could see Geela's approaching Android army. In the distance, she imagined that Geela herself was preparing to torture the people of Athenia. The self-appointed empress had already managed to take control of all the media networks in the galaxy. Today's planetary takeover and attack on the royal families was the next step in her quest for total domination.

Mettathena hustled toward the palace exit, scowling. Her usually stony, powder-gray features were slightly flushed from the stress of the day. Even though she'd had time to prepare for what was to come, she hated sneaking away like some kind of coward.

Since that morning, Mettathena had been aware of the plan for her escape. As she was leaving breakfast— two perfectly poached eggs, served up with a side of political essays—she had overheard her parents on a holo-call with the other royal families of the Pentangle. She had only caught the tail end of the conversation, but that was enough: the planets of the Pentangle were preparing for an attack from the evil empress Geela, and the royal families were all at risk.

The kings and queens of each of the five planets in their galaxy—Athenia, Rhealo, Junoia, Heralda, and Lunaria—had agreed to send the five teenaged princesses away to safety with Chamberlin, the senior butler in Athenia's royal court. He would be tasked with watching over each of the junior royals and keeping them safe until it was safe for them to return to their homes again. As a matter of practicality and courtesy, Chamberlin had been dispatched to fetch the princesses on the other planets first . . . with orders to return for Mettathena as soon as the other girls were secure.

Chamberlin had collected the other four princesses as planned, and now he had returned to collect Mettathena. While she waited to be called away, she had packed a small trunk full of supplies—a dozen sensible black smocks, six pairs of smart pants (one extra in case of spills or stains), and enough clean underwear that each of the princesses would have a week's supply. At the last minute, she threw in five pairs of fleece pajamas—it could be cold where they were going, and she wanted to make sure they would all sleep comfortably. A good night's sleep was the easiest way to keep your wits about you.

She had also tossed in an electric keyboard, to keep herself from going crazy. Princess Mettathena was good at keeping her emotions in check, but she could only keep a level head when she had a few minutes during the day to express herself musically. It was kind of her dirty little secret. She knew her parents would be horrified if they knew about her songwriting, which is why she kept it quiet and private. Mettathena knew the other princesses of the Pentangle had gone through music lessons, too, so she had set a trunk with an electric guitar, a bass guitar, and a pair of drumsticks in the loading dock, hoping the other girls would appreciate the extra courtesy.

Mettathena hurried through the cold, angular corridors of Athenia's palace. Ahead, she spotted Chamberlin waiting for her. He was dressed as a doctor, complete with a heavily starched lab coat and a bag full of medical tools. The butler fell into step beside her and asked, "Ready, Your Highness?"

Mettathena glanced at him. "I suppose. Are you *sure* I must flee? Can't I stay and help the people?"

"No, Your Highness," Chamberlin said under his breath. "Your parents have given me strict orders to take you away. It is for your own safety."

"What about everyone else's safety?" she snapped. The princess stopped to readjust her wig, then bent down to check to see that Mykie was still well hidden. When she looked up again, one of Geela's henchmen was standing right in front of them.

"Who are you?" the large, meaty guard barked.

"Merely lowly servants," Mettathena lied. "A nursery maid. And a palace doctor." She raised her voice an octave, then squeaked, "We are taking this baby to the hospital wing. It is the child of one of the kitchen staff. It had the nerve to *cough* on the princess's breakfast this morning. The royal family has asked me to remove it from the grounds as punishment." The princess felt herself sweating beneath her wig and costume. She hoped her disguise and acting were believable.

The guard peered over the edge of the pram and scowled. "Ugly kid," he noted.

Mykie growled quietly, then sneezed in the guard's face.

"Rude, too," the guard said, narrowing his eyes. "Well . . . the royal family isn't in charge around here anymore, so this kid can cough as much as it likes."

Mettathena's eyes widened. She snuck a quick glance at Chamberlin, who refused to look at her. "What do you mean?" she asked.

"I mean," the guard said, barking out a laugh. "The king and queen are already in the glorious and all-powerful Empress Geela's possession. They've been taken to a secret location. Now we just need to find and capture that princess brat." He looked over Mettathena's shoulder and peered down the hallway. "If you see her, send her my way. We get a bonus from the empress if we deliver her a princess."

Mettathena held her breath as the guard hustled away. Then, without further discussion, she and Chamberlin raced off in the opposite direction before anyone else could stop and talk to them. Although Princess Mettathena had never been one to show her emotions, she felt a lump of sadness forming in her throat—her parents had been taken prisoner, and her planet was in turmoil. Life in their usually peaceful galaxy was about to change.

But by the time she, Mykie, and Chamberlin reached the old space transport that would take them to safety, she had managed to shove her sadness and fear aside. Crying wouldn't get her anywhere. If she ever wanted to get her planet back, Mettathena knew she would have to be smart and composed. She was ready: it was time to fight back. She just had to figure out how she was going to do that.

She stepped inside the transport, slid the wig off her head, and looked at the four other girls sitting inside. "Hello, Your Highnesses. Let's get started."

CHAPTER 1

"THIS PLANET IS A TOTAL SPACE DUMP," PRINCESS Lunaria announced, regally stepping off the space transport onto Borana's litter-strewn streets. The princess of Lunaria stood on her tiptoes, trying to keep most of her feet from touching the filthy ground. Her pet, Adora, whimpered to be picked up. She curled into a tight ball in the princess's arms. Adora detested soiled paws.

"On the bright side," Princess Rhealetta muttered. "We're not in one of Geela's prisons, or worse. So there's that."

Lunaria glared at her. The only "bright side," as far as she was concerned, was that the atmosphere of Borana seemed to be somewhat humid—so at least her skin would stay dewy while they were on their little holiday.

None of the other princesses said anything, but it was clear from the looks on each of their faces that every one of them was thinking the same thing—Borana was really, truly nasty. This was a major step down from their home planets. The ground was dull gray and pock-marked; piles of garbage and recycled metals were heaped up all over the place. The sky was stormy and mustard yellow, and the smell of the air had a definite funk to it.

But the fact was, there weren't any lovely resort planets where five princesses on the run could hide—and there hadn't been a lot of time to plan—so Chamberlin had taken the best and only option available to them. Sitting just outside the Pentangle Galaxy, Borana was close enough that the five girls hadn't had to fly for months to get there. But it was also obscure and remote enough that no one would ever come looking for them.

"Well," Chamberlin said in a strangely chipper voice. It had been a long ride with the shuttle full of young princesses, and he was eager to put his feet up and prepare a cup of tea. "Shall we get settled? Unpack? See the sights?"

The five princesses all glared at him. Chamberlin's smile slipped. "Right, then." He cleared his throat and clapped once, briskly. "First order of business: we need to come up with new names for all of you. I realize Borana is, well . . . a bit out of the way and rather lightly populated. But I don't want to risk using your real names from now on, just in case."

He looked first at Junoia and said, "We'll keep this simple. From now on, you will be called Juno."

Juno shrugged. "Fine by me. Whatever floats your boat."

"Princess Mettathena," Chamberlin said, bowing slightly. "Henceforth, you shall be known as Athena."

Athena nodded. "Very well."

"And you," he said, turning to Herazanna. "We will shorten your name to Hera."

"Heeeee-ra," Hera said, stretching her new name out. Roxie, her little fluffball pet, bounced up and down happily. "I love it!" She giggled and looked to the other girls for approval. "Soothing, isn't it?"

"Like a warm, sudsy bath," Rhealetta muttered. She grinned at Chamberlin. "Lemme guess my new name, Chamberlin. Could it be . . . Rhea?"

"Very good," Chamberlin said, surprised. "How did you know?"

Rhea chuckled. "Lucky guess."

Chamberlin smiled thinly at Lunaria, who scowled back. The two of them hadn't exactly gotten off on the right foot. And now that Lunaria's feet and ankles were covered in dark gray Borana dust, she looked even feistier than she had earlier in the day. "And you, miss—" he began.

"*Princess* Lunaria will be just fine," Lunaria said, cutting him off. She crossed her arms and announced, "I am *not* changing my name. No one is going to recognize me without lipstick anyway, and since you wouldn't let me pack any of my makeup before stuffing me into that laundry basket . . . well, there is absolutely no need for me to change my name."

"I'm afraid we must," Chamberlin said. "You shall be known as Luna from this moment on. And speaking of makeup—"

"You have makeup?!" Luna shrieked. She thrust out a hand and wiggled it under Chamberlin's nose. "I order you to hand it over to me, right this moment."

Chamberlin cleared his throat again.

"You've been clearing your throat all day. Do you have something stuck in there?" Rhea asked with a jaunty tilt of her head. "If your throat is scratchy, maybe Luna would be willing to share some of her juice with you."

"As if," Luna snapped. "I am a princess. I. Don't. *Share*. Juice."

Chamberlin stepped between the two girls. "As I was saying, we will also need to outfit you all with disguises.

I do not have traditional makeup, but we do need to discuss how to make each of you up so you look somewhat different. Your parents packed a trunk with some basic supplies, such as hair dye, wigs, and accessories. Obviously, without those, you are each highly recognizable. Geela has an impressive army searching for you, and we need to make finding you as difficult as possible."

The princesses studied one another carefully. Each of the five planets of the Pentangle had highly different fashions, and every one of the royal courts had different ideas about how nobility ought to dress. Hera's flowing skirt and flowered shirt were a far cry from Athena's prim navy blue jumper and turtleneck. Luna's fussy dress seemed galaxies away from Juno's drab exercise uniform. And Rhea's buttoned-up, angled tunic was just plain odd. It was clear from the raised eyebrows and quiet snickers that each of the girls thought the others' outfits were utterly tragic.

Athena stepped forward. In a matter-of-fact voice, she announced, "I have good news. I brought changes of clothes for everyone. I planned ahead, assuming we would all want to get out of our travel clothes when we arrived." She gestured to Chamberlin, who pulled Athena's trunk full of supplies out of the space transport. The princess of Athenia opened the trunk, then handed each of her fellow princesses a matching outfit.

Juno's eyes went wide. She held up a pair of neatly hemmed, conservative blue pants. "You're kidding, right?"

Athena blinked. "About what?"

"You want us to wear *this*?" Rhea asked, waving a smock in the air. "This . . . thing?"

"I also brought several changes of underwear for each of you," Athena said, not understanding the looks the other girls were giving her. "I hope they are the right size."

Luna's mouth hung open. "You brought us *underwear*? You expect me to wear someone else's used underwear?"

"They're clean!" Athena said. "Why are you all look-ing at me like this is a bad thing?"

"I think Athena's clothes are cute," Hera said. She was busy wrapping the tunic around her pet. She crooned, "Doesn't she look absolutely adorable in this shirt? It suits you, Roxie . . . yes it does! Yes, it does!"

Juno and Rhea both glanced at Chamberlin. "You're not going to make us wear these clothes from Mettathena—I mean, Athena, are you?" Juno blurted out. Skitter grunted her agreement.

"They're awful," Rhea announced.

"I have a few spare clothes here, too," Luna said. "Chamberlin had to sneak me out of the castle inside my laundry basket this morning. There are a few gowns inside my laundry that might work for disguises."

"I'd rather be caught by Geela," Juno said, "than be caught dead in one of your dresses."

"Perhaps now is not the time to discuss your disguises," Chamberlin said diplomatically. "Shall we work on getting you all settled first?"

"Where is the hotel bellhop?" Luna said. She waved her arm in the air and yelled, "Hel-*lo!* Can we get some service over here?"

"Take a look around," Rhea said, rolling her eyes. "Doesn't look like there are a whole lot of servants wandering around on this garbage dump of a planet."

"Oh, but there must be bellhops," Luna said, laughing. "What proper hotel would make a princess carry her own bag? Even chain hotels have staff."

"And where *is* the hotel?" Athena asked.

The five spoiled teenage princesses all looked to Chamberlin for an answer. "There is no hotel," he said. "No palace, no castle, no servants, no bellhops. Only me, this space transport, and the five of you. And your pets, of course. We'll all be bunking together in here." He gestured to the vehicle they had used for their escape, which suddenly looked even smaller than it had felt on the ride out to Borana. "It will be cozy."

Reluctantly, the five princesses stepped back into the transport and took in their surroundings with fresh eyes. The space transport was large and roomy, shaped like an old-fashioned tour bus. There was one big room that looked and felt like a living room in the center of the ship. This is where the girls had relaxed and started getting to know one another on their journey out to Borana.

Now, they moved beyond the main room and explored the rest of the transport. At the front of the ship were a modern kitchen and dining area, as well as the control room for the vehicle. At the far end of the ship were two bedrooms. One was tiny and windowless, the size of one of Luna's walk-in closets. The walls were bare and painted a dull gray. "This room is mine," Chamberlin explained.

The other room was large and spacious, about the size of each of the princesses' bedrooms back home. It had one big hangout area in the middle, surrounded by five separate sleeping pods. Each pod was sparsely decorated.

"You can each design your space to your liking," Chamberlin said hopefully.

The girls poked their heads into the pods, not bothering to hide their disgust.

The floors were stark and cold, but there was a sofa and five pet beds clustered together in the center of the hangout area that helped make it look more homey.

Without hesitation, each of the princesses' pets raced forward and claimed a bed, then snuggled in for much-needed afternoon naps.

"Look! All our pets are already becoming best friends!" Hera cried happily.

"The bestest," Rhea said in a sarcastic voice.

After a quick glance at one another, the five girls all ran into the room and began fighting for turf. "I call this pod!" Luna screamed, shoving Hera aside to get to the pod on one end of the room before any of the other girls could claim it.

Rhea hastily grabbed the pod at the other end of the room. Juno settled in beside her. Athena took the sleeping pod in the middle of them all, and Hera floated toward the only one that was left. She flopped down on her bed, bounced a few times, and announced, "This is going to be so fun! Like a giant sleepover! I've seen movies about sleepovers," she said, frowning. "But I've never had one."

In fact, none of the girls had ever had a sleepover. None of them had shared a room or argued over a bed in their lives. They had never listened to the sounds of someone else snoring nearby, or made their own bed in the morning, or slept under a blanket that hadn't been custom-made for a princess.

"Where are all the closets?" Luna asked, stepping out of her pod and scanning the area. "Where is *my* closet?"

"Does it matter?" Rhea snapped at her. "The only clothes you have are the ones you're wearing and a few nasty dresses inside your hamper. Why would you need a closet?"

Luna choked back a sob as the grim reality of their situation hit her. "And the servants?" she asked.

Athena shook her head once.

"The chefs?" Luna asked, gulping. "The gardener? My chambermaid?"

"We've got Chamber*lin*," Rhea pointed out helpfully.

Hera reached toward Luna and rubbed her back. "It will all work out," she promised. "We just need to keep a positive attitude."

"How about you feed your positive attitude to a space rat?" Juno said, her words coming out a little more harshly than she'd intended them to. "I, for one, have no interest in sitting here braiding each other's hair and pretending that nothing is wrong."

No one said anything. For many long minutes, the room was silent. Suddenly, a tinny blast of music broke through the quiet. Four heads swiveled around to glare at Luna. She had her communicator out and was streaming a cheesy love ballad at full volume.

Luna shrugged and said, "What? If we're stuck on this horrible planet, we might as well have music." She flopped back onto the couch and sang along.

The other girls shared surprised looks—Luna could *sing*. And clearly, she knew it. She was singing loudly enough for half the planet to hear her. Even though the song sounded good, after a few verses, the silly lyrics began to grate on the other girls. "Can you turn it down?" Athena asked.

"Nope," Luna said with a shrug.

"That wasn't actually a question," Athena said. "What I meant to say is, 'turn it down!'"

Luna acted like she hadn't heard her.

Before they could argue about it further, Chamberlin raced into the room. "What *is* that ruckus?" he shouted over the music.

"'Sprinkle of Roses,'" Luna said. "You are seriously out of touch, Chambermaid. It was number three on the Galaxy Top Twelve last week. And if Geela hadn't taken over the radio stations, it would have climbed to number one this week."

Chamberlin massaged his temples. "But where is the sound *coming* from?"

Luna wiggled her communicator in the air. "This adorable little box is called a communicator," she said slowly as if speaking to a toddler, explaining the obvious. "The inhabitants of my planet use it for ordering takeout, listening to music, watching TV, booking their spa appointments, and sending messages."

Chamberlin groaned. "Give it to me."

"Excuse me?" Luna growled.

"Geela could be using your communicator to track you," Chamberlin explained. "How many of you have communication devices with you right now?"

One by one, each of the girls raised their hands. "*Obviously*, that's all of us," Rhea said. "I don't go anywhere without mine."

In a flash, Chamberlin reached into the nearest pod and grabbed the pillow off Juno's bed. He shook the pillow out of its pillowcase and held the case out toward the girls. "Drop them in," he ordered. "All devices in here, no exceptions. From now on, you are to have no communication with the outside world. No devices that might help Geela track you to Borana. No social media, no messaging, no interaction with anyone except your fellow princesses and me. Period. Got it?"

The girls nodded solemnly.

Although it hurt to have their contact with the outside world severed, the princesses all knew Chamberlin had a point. Their communicators were equipped with technology that could easily bring in unwanted attention. One wrong move and Geela would be after them again.

With a minimal amount of whining, they each threw their devices into the pillowcase. Then they trailed along after him and watched—horrified—as Chamberlin threw their devices into the ship's incinerator. The fire raged, shooting out blue and purple sparks as the girls' devices—and the internal chips, trackers, and memories—were melted and destroyed.

It was necessary, but that didn't mean it was any less difficult to say goodbye. Without their communicators, the five girls now had no way of connecting with the outside world, no way of keeping up on fashion or gossip, and no way of ordering clothes or takeout.

And to make matters worse, Juno no longer had a pillowcase. Life outside the Pentangle Galaxy was neither fun nor fair.

CHAPTER 2

LATE THAT NIGHT, LONG AFTER CHAMBERLIN'S usual bedtime, all five girls, the assortment of pets, and their butler were all camped out on the couches in their space transport's living room. Because there was nothing else to do—no communicators, no media players, no elegant dinners, no royal obligations—the six of them were lounging around watching the only holo-screen Chamberlin had installed on board. It wasn't the way any of them would usually choose to spend their free time, but it was better than staring at a blank wall. Sort of.

"This is all garbage," Athena said, flicking her finger across the enormous 3D images to change from one show to another. Her finger paused and she jumped back from the hologram when she landed on the Geela Romance Network. She scowled at the figure in the center of the living room. For there, in the middle of them all, was a life-size hologram of Empress Geela wearing a long black shift dress, her cruel mouth set in an unconvincing smile. *"The Empress?"* Athena scoffed. "Is she serious?"

"She's trying to find love on a reality show," Rhea explained. The girls all stared at the hologram, transfixed, as a good-looking alien wearing a tuxedo and metallic space helmet materialized beside Geela. The empress linked arms with him, then led her date toward a sleek transport, telling him that they would be having dinner on the planet Tik-Tik tonight.

"Who would want to go on a date with her?" Luna wondered aloud. "She's awful."

Juno, who had been doing crunches on the floor, kicked at the empress's lifelike figure and said, "Isn't a reality show the perfect place for an evil empress to find her soul mate? She controls the network, so I'm sure she can figure out some way to get at least one of these guys to fall in love with her."

Athena flicked her hand to change the channel again, landing next on an all-day marathon of *Geela's Rocky*

Remodel. Geela was in the process of remodeling her fortress, and the renovation show took viewers inside her massive home as construction crews demolished and redesigned the spaces to her very bizarre specifications.

On PBC—the Pentangle Broadcast Corporation—a new episode of *Dancing with the Empress* was just wrapping up. Geela had earned perfect tens across the board for her swing, space-crunk, and tango performances. The audience, which was made up of the empress's paid employees, clapped wildly as she took a bow and collected her trophy. As soon as the credits rolled (*Executive Producer: Geela, Director: Geela, Creative Director: Geela, Wardrobe Supervisor: Geela*), an episode of *Cooking with G!* began. "Tonight," the host announced, "Geela will be making meteor meat stew! Yum yum!"

Athena angrily jabbed at a button on the bottom of the device, and the hologram of the empress melted away. "How did she manage to take over half the galaxy?" she griped. "All these shows are either about Geela's life or house or hobbies, or they actually *star* her!"

"Half?" Rhea said. "More like all. She controls *all* of the television stations and every single one of the production companies now. She also pays off the music networks to be sure they don't say or sing anything bad about her. She's taken over the entire galaxy's media outlets. And now she's taken over control of our people, too."

Hera sighed. "I miss my favorite show, *Meditation with Tranla*. It was such a relaxing way to end the day."

"Yeah, well," Juno snapped. "Now you'll get to meditate with Geela and her Android army. There's no way the cold-hearted empress is going to let a fruity-tooty character like Tranla teach meditation on one of the networks she's controlling."

"Tranla is *not* fruity-tooty!" Hera said. She pursed her lips into a scowl and folded her feet up under her body. "She's inspiring! Just because you don't take the time to reflect and turn off the noise, it doesn't mean meditation is not a beautiful thing." Suddenly, she brightened. "Hey, how about I lead all of you in a short guided relaxation session right now?"

"Dream on, Hera," Juno laughed. "I'm more of a pull-up and crunch kind of girl. Keeping physically strong is the only thing that's really going to help when it's time to fight back against Geela."

"Fight back against Geela?" Chamberlin blurted out, chuckling nervously. He shifted and took a sip of tea, but spit it back into the mug when he realized his drink had gone cold. He missed the stay-warm mugs he had had back at the palace. "Don't be silly. We have no plans to fight. Our job is to wait in safety and then return when all of the danger has passed. Get comfy, young ladies. We could be here for a while."

"You want us to just sit here on *Bore*-ana and do nothing while our families and people are under attack from that evil empress?" Juno growled. "I think it's you who's being silly."

"Yeah," Athena said. "Geela has taken over our planets, she's controlling all the media in the entire galaxy, and she's trying to brainwash the inhabitants of the Pentangle that she's some kind of amazing leader, masterful dancer, and celebrity chef. But all she is . . . is a tyrant! It's totally insane. She's not a hero!"

"Totally. *We* are the heroes. The people of our planets should be looking up to us, the royalty," Luna said. "*Dancing with Princesses* would make a much better show. Obviously."

Rhea shook her head. "I don't think that's quite what Athena and Juno were trying to say, Luna. We want the people of our galaxy to be free to watch the shows they want to watch, and to listen to the music they love, and to live in freedom—not cower in fear under Geela's controlling thumb. Anyway, how can we be considered heroes when we all ran away from our homes and our people at the first sign of danger?"

"This discussion has gone far enough," Chamberlin

said, standing up. "As I've explained to each of you, the kings and queens of the Pentangle came up with their plan to evacuate the five of you before Geela took over your planets. They all agreed that it is paramount to keep you hidden. If Geela were to find you . . ." He trailed off. "Well, it would be a very bad thing indeed. Dangerous, dangerous." He shook his head and scowled.

"I guess we'll just have to agree to disagree, Chamberlin," Juno said. "I'm going to fight, and there's not much you can do about it."

"This is not a fight for five young girls," he announced, stomping his foot. "You are princesses. *Royalty.* You are duty-bound to act in a way that is appropriate to your title."

"You did *not* just say that!" Juno snarled. Chamberlin cowered under her fierce gaze.

Athena crossed her arms and scowled at her long-standing butler. "How can you tell us what kind of behavior is appropriate to our title when everything about our world has just changed?"

"Are you saying that princesses are supposed to sit on a throne and look pretty?" Rhea scoffed. "Because that would be a seriously boring life."

"Is looking pretty really such a bad thing?" Luna asked under her breath.

Hera broke in, "We need to be strong for our people.

We need to protect them, and ensure that the world is safe and happy. If that means I need to fight back against Geela, that's what I'll do." Then she looked at Chamberlin and added, "But I don't want to hurt anyone's feelings."

Grumbling, Chamberlin turned and shuffled toward his bedroom. "This conversation is over," he declared. It was becoming increasingly clear to the old butler that he was very much out of his league. Five teenage princesses—all of whom were used to getting their way—were obviously more than one old butler could handle. *Ah well,* he thought, slipping into bed. He was the only one who knew the code that would start the transport. Unless they tricked him somehow, no one was going anywhere or fighting anything.

He slid his dark eye mask down over his face, trying to tune out the sound of the girls bickering in the bedroom next to his own. He could hear Luna ordering the other girls to fetch a glass of warm milk for her. Chamberlin chuckled. These young ladies would have to get used to a whole new way of life out here on Borana—and fast, or he would very likely fail his mission.

But Chamberlin knew better than anyone that failure was not an option. He had promised the kings and queens of the Pentangle that he would watch over the princesses and protect them with his life. Months away from retirement, and he had been given the most difficult challenge of his career.

Just as Luna's angry footsteps stormed down the hall toward the kitchen, Chamberlin drifted off to sleep, hoping the morning would bring sunshine, a ship full of happy and easygoing girls, and some much-needed relaxation.

CHAPTER 3

"I'M NEXT," LUNA ANNOUNCED, PUSHING PAST Chamberlin to step into the only bathroom on board the space transport. The bathroom door whooshed closed, leaving Chamberlin alone in the chilly hallway. The butler sighed and returned to his room, bath caddy hanging loosely by his side.

Chamberlin had been waiting to get in the shower for several hours, and every time he thought it was finally his turn, one of the girls beat him to the bathroom door. The shower had been running for nearly four hours straight. He was beginning to suspect that when he finally got his chance to wash up, there would be no hot water left.

As far as Chamberlin was concerned, the first morning on Borana had been nothing short of a disaster. Juno was the first girl awake, at the stroke of five-thirty. As was her morning custom, Juno turned on loud, angry music and launched into a workout. Of course, the music had woken up the other girls, who were less than pleased about the early wake-up call. There had been a lot of groaning and yelling—and several thrown shoes.

Rhea and Luna both preferred to stay up late and sleep in, so five-thirty was an unacceptable hour in their minds. (And Luna, of course, was upset about not having her customary morning juice delivered for the second morning in a row.) Hera didn't particularly mind waking up early, but Juno's grunting and blood-pumping music had gotten in the way of her relaxing sun salutations and rosehip tea. Athena was indifferent about the time on the clock, but she hated not having her privacy first thing in the morning. She hated people seeing her in her vulnerable, just-awake condition.

As soon as it was clear that no one would be getting back to sleep, the girls began fighting over the shower. Then there had been a slew of arguments about whose job it was to clean up after breakfast. Every one of them left their dishes on the table when they had finished eating, obviously expecting that the mess would magically disappear and be dealt with. The girls' room was already messy, and Hera had reluctantly informed the others that she didn't know how to tie her own shoes (someone had always done it for her).

The constant bickering had gotten louder and louder as the morning went on, and the smell in the kitchen began to seep out into the common rooms. Lunch was still hours away, and every single one of them was on their very last nerve. They hadn't been together for twenty-four hours, and it already felt like an eternity.

Early in the afternoon, as a treat and an attempt at distraction, Chamberlin had opened up the crates of supplies and disguises he had brought along for the girls. "These are just some things that will help get us through until you can all return home," he explained. Inside the crates they found a random collection of clothing and fabric, kits of hair dye, crafting supplies, a dozen pairs of ratty shoes and boots, and several very out-of-date music players.

The girls removed everything from the boxes and laid it out in the transport's living room. "Ugly, uglier, and ugliest," Luna said, surveying the selection of clothing with a scowl on her face. "Where and when did you get this stuff, Chamberlin? Were all of these things in some sort of Borana grade school lost-and-found bin back in 2016?"

Chamberlin frowned at her. "I did the best that I could. You may choose outfits from this supply or wear the clothes that Athena brought for you. The only thing you need to know is, you will no longer be allowed to dress in your usual clothing."

"Some of these things are sort of pretty," Hera said, pulling out a length of silver fabric. She rubbed the fabric against her face and said, "This feels like evening bramble rose petals!" With a sunny smile, she added, "And it will be nice to have some music to listen to."

Rhea dug around at the bottom of the box and extracted a sewing kit. She grinned, holding the kit up like a prize. "Anyone care if I tear this stuff up and make it look like it came from a store instead of the trash? I can make a few alterations to everything and it might be halfway decent. I could totally design a cute disguise for each of us." She looked at each of the other princesses and added, "I think I can come up with something that will suit each of your styles, but that is just far enough from your regular clothes that we'll all look really different. I learned to sew when I was nine. It was part of my formal princess training—but making all those silly quilts and skirts was immensely dull, so I convinced my tutors to let me study fashion design instead. I practiced my skills on the palace employees."

"Go for it," Juno said, glancing skeptically at a long purple skirt with butterflies embroidered on it. "Good luck."

Athena nodded. "If you are qualified, then by all means, have at it."

Rhea gathered all the clothes up into her arms—the drab selection from Athena and the random hand-me-downs from Chamberlin—and headed for the girls' bedroom, happy to have a little solo project to keep her busy for a while.

Meanwhile, Chamberlin dismissed himself for a much-needed nap. Muttering something about a tepid shower and not enough sleep, he shuffled off. The girls' butler was obviously disappointed no one had appreciated his little gift.

As soon as he was gone, Athena slid her trunk of supplies out. The clothes she had packed hadn't been popular with the other girls, but she hoped the other things would be. She pulled out the musical instruments, one by one. As soon as her keyboard was settled on her lap, Athena spread out her fingers and played a few notes. Something about the bright sound of the keys carried her straight back home, to the only planet and life she had ever known. Playing the keyboard made her feel at home.

"Drumsticks!" Juno gasped, peering into the trunk. She pulled them out, her purple face bright. "May I?"

"Of course," Athena said. "I brought these things to share. But I don't have any drums . . ."

Juno grinned. "That's not a problem. This planet is a space dump, remember? I'm sure there are some things floating around outside that I can use to put together a kit." She raced toward the door of the space transport, certain she could build a killer drum set out of spare parts and recycled metals on the streets of Borana.

Hera reached into the trunk and tugged out the bass guitar. She flopped back onto the couch and strummed a few notes. She closed her eyes and relaxed into the sound. She, too, felt most at home with an instrument— or her camera—in her hands.

"You play bass?" Luna asked, sounding both surprised and impressed.

"A little," Hera shrugged. She plucked at the strings. "I'm more of a classical upright bass player, but an electric bass can be pretty fun from time to time, too. Do you play any instruments, Luna?"

"I've been taking vocal lessons for thirteen years," Luna boasted. "Opera, French classical, and soprano ballads are my specialties. I write songs and play a little piano, too—but only because my tutors made me learn so I would be a 'well-rounded' princess."

Athena tapped out a simple melody on her keyboard. A few notes in, Luna began to sing along:

Livin' on Borana.
It doesn't get a whole lot uglier than this.
But life . . . as we know it . . . is gone, gone, gone.
Lost. Forgotten. Stolen . . .

Her voice cut out. But a moment later, Hera jumped in and filled in the empty spaces with the thrumming beat of her bass.

Rhea peeked out of the bedroom, her face lighting up when she saw the unused electric guitar on top of Athena's trunk. She bopped out to the living room, strapped it over her shoulder, and chimed in. For a few minutes, the girls were unified in song. For once, they were getting along—but only because they didn't have to talk.

The tranquility only lasted for a few minutes. Just as Luna had started building a new verse, Juno returned to the space transport with a collection of metal to create her drum kit. She spread all the supplies out in the living room, crashing and banging around and taking no notice of the other girls. It was as if she were totally unaware that she was making a ruckus.

Irritated, Luna snapped, "I can't hear myself think with you building your noisy little toys over there. Can you *please* go somewhere else?" She said this in a voice that suggested she was used to getting what she asked—always.

"These are not toys," Juno grunted. "It's gonna be a killer set of drums."

Luna rolled her eyes. "Whatever. Drums are just noise-makers. They don't make real music. You and your stack of garbage over there are ruining my sound."

Juno glared at her but said nothing. She returned to her project, tapping her drumstick against one of the drums in a thrumming rhythm. It actually sounded great.

"I just had an idea," Athena said suddenly. "What if we all tried to play together? Like a band?"

"Backup for me?" Luna clarified.

"As if," Rhea scoffed. "A band is a group thing. There is no star."

"Unless you're the singer," Luna said. "A band's singer is *obviously* the star. It's the words that matter. The instruments are just background noise."

The other girls began to argue with her, but Athena put up a hand to silence them all. Miraculously, the bickering stopped. "Every member of a band is important. And since we all play different instruments, we could make an amazing group." She put her hands on her hips. "At least it's something to *do*."

Juno looked up from her makeshift drum kit and muttered, "So I'm not allowed to fight back against Geela . . . but I am allowed to play cute little songs with a bunch of princesses? *Awesome.*"

"It *is* awesome," Hera said, not realizing Juno was being sarcastic.

"What if we did both?" Athena said. "Chamberlin won't let us fight back against Geela as ourselves—but what if we fought back through music?"

Rhea shook her head. "I'm not following."

"We could write rebellion songs!" Athena said, her usually pale cheeks flushed pink. "Here's what I'm thinking: We go undercover as a band and get our songs broadcast to spread the message of hope and rebellion."

"And love. I'd love to spread a message of love," Hera cooed.

"But we can't broadcast anything," Juno pointed out. "Every station is all Geela all the time." Quietly, she added, "I wonder when *she'll* form a band . . ."

"So I guess we just have to go out on tour, then," Rhea said, shrugging.

Athena pointed at her. "Yes! We can travel around the galaxy preaching a message of rebellion, freedom, *and* love to the people!"

"I'm all about rebellion," Juno agreed.

"If you think we can help our people and planets reclaim their freedom, I'm in!" Rhea said happily.

"I'd be the lead singer of this band, right?" Luna asked. She looked around at the other girls, waiting for them to agree. No one replied, so Luna continued, "As long as I don't have to share the spotlight with anyone, I guess I'll do it."

"A band," Athena said, nodding. "I like it."

Rhea grinned. "Geela is always bashing other peoples' music, so what better way to rebel against her than by writing a bunch of freedom songs?"

"I can think of a few better ways to get back at Geela," Juno said, punching a fist into her palm. She pounded one of her drumsticks noisily against the edge of her homemade cymbal.

"*Nonviolent* fighting," Hera said softly. "This is the smart way to fight."

"I have to say, your idea is kind of brilliant, Athena," Luna noted with a small smile.

Juno shrugged and said, "I'm in, too. Just know that I'll be pretending my snare drum is Geela's starship." Then she lifted her arm high and slammed one of her drumsticks down with an enormous boom. The fight was on.

CHAPTER 4

"THE MOST IMPORTANT PART OF FORMING A BAND is costumes," Luna announced. "If we want to be taken seriously, we absolutely have to look the part."

"That's the most important thing?" Rhea asked, lifting an eyebrow. "Really? More than the music?"

"Of course!" Luna insisted. "If we start touring, and then we get super famous—because of my voice, of course—and sell T-shirts with my face on them and . . ." She broke off, momentarily distracted by the thought of T-shirts with her own face on them scattered far and wide across the galaxy. "Well, everyone will recognize me unless I look seriously different."

"She's right," Athena said, stepping into the hall to

make sure Chamberlin's white noise machine was still cranked up nice and loud. The girls had discovered their butler preferred to sleep with relaxing Heralda lute music playing in the background. "Just like Chamberlin has been telling us since we got to Borana, we're going to need clever disguises. I think our new names are different enough, but our looks need a major overhaul. Especially if we think we're going to play gigs and be in front of crowds."

"Of course we're going to play gigs! For huge crowds!" Luna scoffed. "Do you have any idea how many connections I have? We can book any club in the galaxy if I just say the word. I'm not at all worried about getting plenty of publicity and attention."

Athena shook her head. "But we can't use your connections. We need to stay in disguise at all times, and we can never tell anyone who we really are."

"We're gonna need to build this band from the ground up," Juno pointed out. "We have to get people to notice our sound without using any royal connections."

"That sounds like a lot of work," Luna said. But after a moment's consideration, she added, "But I'm sure we can get plenty of people to pay attention to us even without connections. I mean, have you *heard* my voice?"

Hera smiled serenely. "I just love that we're going to build something together, sisters. Just think—yesterday morning, we only knew of each other. Now, we are forming a beautiful band and preparing to spread a message of love to the people of our galaxy as a group of friends. I wish I had my camera so I could capture this moment! Can we have a big group hug instead?"

"Oh my Grock," Rhea griped. "We're not going to be that kind of band, are we? Let's just take group hugs off the table right now. Anyone else agree?"

Athena raised her hand. Juno snorted and turned away.

"Now that we've gotten the hugging issue out of the way, what should we do first?" Juno asked. "Want to try to play something? It kind of seems like we should make sure this band thing is going to work before we waste any time on elaborate rock star makeovers."

The other girls all agreed to jam for a bit before getting too deep into their costume design. So a few minutes later, they had assembled their instruments in the bedroom to play for a small, furry crowd made up of the five princesses' pets.

They made sure the door to their room was sealed tight so they didn't wake Chamberlin. Then Juno counted off: "One, two, one, two, three, four!" In a storm of sound, they all began to play. It was a mess of twangs, clanks, and screeching voices. No one was in the same key, they were all over the place on style, and Luna had already begun to cry. Every one of the pets raced for cover under the couch.

"You all sound terrible!" Luna screamed, slamming down the hairbrush she had been using as a microphone.

"Let's try that again," Athena said patiently. "This time, we'll try it in the key of C. Juno, you start. Then Hera, you can come in next. Rhea, you and I can try to jump in on keyboard and guitar after those two have laid down the beat. And then—" She looked pointedly at Luna. "Then, you can try to lay some lyrics over the top. Okay?"

"Fine," Luna said, sighing.

This time, they were all a little more in sync. But almost as soon as Luna had come in with a crooning "Ooh-ooh-wa!" Juno launched into a drum solo that drowned the rest of them out.

"Let's try it again," Athena said, waving her hand in the air. "This isn't the time to show off what we can do. We're trying to make something work as a group. Be mindful of what we sound like together."

Over and over, the girls tried—and failed—to make their styles mesh together. After more than an hour of clashing and fighting, they all agreed it was best to take a break. "We'll get it," Athena assured the others. "It's not going to happen in one afternoon."

"Yeah," Rhea agreed. "Let's take a rest, then try again."

"Should we all share a truth?" Hera suggested.

"A truth?" Juno asked.

"Something secret about ourselves. To help us all get

to know one another better." Hera shrugged. "Sometimes, when creatures can connect on a spiritual level by sharing something personal, it helps to connect them in other ways, too."

"Let's save secret telling for bedtime," Rhea suggested. "We can each wear a pair of those soft fluffy jammies that Athena brought for us from Athenia, and share a quiet secret before we drift off to dreamland." She grinned. "How about we do makeovers now instead? Let's look inside the box of makeup and hair stuff our parents sent and see what kind of changes we can make that will help us look the part. At least then we're making some progress on getting the band up and running."

"I'll go first!" Luna said quickly. She stood in front of the others, and said, "I'm ready for a change."

The other girls studied her. Luna's golden skin was offset by floor-length reddish hair. Her dramatic hair would make her stand out in any crowd.

"I think we need to go bold," Rhea said, circling her. "I want to cut your hair and give you swooping bangs. Then I think we should add highlights. If we put in a ton of golden streaks, your hair would really accent your skin color beautifully."

Luna looked at herself in the mirror hanging from the wall. She ran her fingers down the length of her hair, then took a breath and said, "Do it."

So Rhea grabbed a pair of scissors from the box and got to work. While Athena and Juno mixed up a box of bleach, Hera and Rhea cut and trimmed Luna's hair so it curled around her hips and fell in a gentle swoop across her forehead. Rhea applied the bleach, then moved on to Athena while they waited for Luna's hair to change.

"With your smooth gray skin and light blue eyes," Rhea said, studying Athena, "I think we need to abandon your fair hair. I'm thinking we give you a bold pop of color—and do something dramatic with your style. Can you handle that?"

Athena nodded briskly. "If I must. Are you thinking nice, sensible brown hair?"

Rhea shook her head.

"Beige?"

Rhea shook her head again.

"Pale peach?"

Rhea grinned. "Pink. No one is going to recognize you if you have hot pink hair. Am I right?"

Athena gaped at her. "You're not serious?"

"Totally. You're going to look amazing," Rhea promised. Before Athena could object or question her further, Rhea lifted her scissors and snipped a huge chunk of hair off Athena's head. She said, "You're going to adore short hair. And the color will be a really fun change."

Next, it was Juno's turn. Juno scowled as Rhea looked her over. Juno's skin was a beautiful, rich purple—a darker version of her eye color. Her hair was forest green, and Juno kept it pulled back in a tight ponytail.

"You can handle bold, yeah?" Rhea asked her.

"Of course," Juno said, jutting her chin out.

"Do you trust me?" Rhea tested.

"Not really," Juno admitted. "I don't trust anyone. But after what you've done to those two, I'm more inclined to test your styling skills."

"Excellent," laughed Rhea. "We're cutting your hair super short and spiky. And I want it to match your skin color. Let's really play up your purple punk style. Okay?"

Juno nodded. "Do it."

Rhea shaved the sides of Juno's head, then gave Luna and Athena instructions on how to dye her hair purple. Meanwhile, she turned her attention to Hera.

"Hera, Hera . . ." she said, studying the kind, pink-skinned sweetheart. Hera's hair was fluffy and soft, and frizzed around her face like lavender cotton candy. "You, girl, need a little edge if you're going to play the bass. I want to dye your hair black, with sharp bangs across your forehead. We can curl the back, to keep you some-what soft looking."

Hera nodded, her eyes wide. "I'm okay with you cutting it—however you want!—but I really don't want to dye it."

"Why not?" Juno blurted out from across the room. "The rest of us did."

"I prefer a more natural approach to fashion," Hera explained. "I like sun-kissed cheeks and honeycomb lip gloss. Beauty you can find in nature! I don't believe in applying toxic chemicals and poisons to my body. It's not good for the constitution."

"Okay . . ." Rhea said, walking toward their bedroom door. She stepped into the hall and said, "I have another idea. I saw one of the palace stylists do this on Rhealo once. Hopefully I was watching carefully enough that I'm able to do it myself!" She returned a moment later with a jet-black starcumber from the space transport kitchen.

While the other girls watched curiously, Rhea squeezed the black juice from the horn-shaped vegetable into a bowl, mixed it with a few drops of sea squid ink, then held it out for Hera's approval. "Ta-da! Natural hair dye."

Hera and the other girls came closer. Luna pinched her nose closed, jumped back, and groaned, "That smells awful!"

"It doesn't smell like sun buttons," Hera agreed, her eyes beginning to water from the rancid smell of the starcumber mixed with sea squid ink. "But if it's all natural, I won't complain. Are you sure this is going to work?"

The ink and veggie juice combo gelled into a thick, mud-like substance and—once applied—turned Hera's hair into a hard helmet. The smell grew even more powerful the longer it sat on Hera's head. They all kept their distance while the color took hold, trying to escape the putrid stench. Hera smiled through the whole ordeal, promising the others that the temporary discomfort would all be worth it in the end. And she was right!

When they washed and dried Hera's hair, they found it had been dyed a vibrant, beautiful black—and the bold bangs framed her huge gray eyes perfectly. She looked like a completely different girl.

As soon as Rhea had dyed her own hair teal—to match her blue skin—and added a jaunty hat to complete her new look, the girls agreed that they all looked totally different.

Rhea pulled out the outfits she'd started to put together, and they all held the fabrics up to themselves. When the five princesses finally stood together before the mirror, everyone hidden behind their new clothes and flaunting their new hairstyles, the results were incredible. "Well?" Rhea asked, nervously looking around at the other girls. "What do you think? Are we ready to say goodbye to the princesses of the Pentangle . . . and hello to the princesses of pop?"

CHAPTER 5

"OUR NEW BAND NAME IS DEFINITELY SUPER cute," Luna said after dinner that night, while the princesses enjoyed a dessert of Pop Rocks over ice cream. Chamberlin claimed it was a Borana specialty . . . but it was also all they could scrounge up. "The Space Princesses of the Pentangle is adorable and totally catchy when it's shortened to SPACEPOP. But I'm wondering if we want to consider a couple other options? Like *Luna and the SPACEPOP* or *Luna and the—*"

Rhea cut her off. "No."

"No?" Luna snapped. "Who made you the boss?"

Chamberlin, who had been busy clearing away the

dinner dishes, looked across the kitchen with a start. "What's this now? A band?"

Athena nodded and said matter-of-factly, "Yes, we've decided to form a rock band."

"The five of you?" Chamberlin asked, his voice getting shrill. "A band?"

"You have a problem with that?" Juno said, raising an eyebrow.

"I most certainly *do* have a problem with that," Chamberlin said, fumbling as he loaded the dishes into the transport's wash pod. "What is the point?"

Hera explained, "We all feel really helpless just sitting here on Borana while that meanie Geela holds our planets and parents hostage. We want to do something to help. To inspire our people."

"I've already told you, the most important thing you can do to help your people is keep yourselves safe," Chamberlin said, clearing his throat—then he cleared it again. The girls had begun to grow fond of some of Chamberlin's nervous tics.

"We're going to go crazy—and possibly kill each other—if we just sit here in this space transport for the next however many months and do nothing," Juno said. "So the other princesses and I have been talking, and we've decided that we're going to go out on tour. We want to write songs that will inspire people to take action. Freedom songs."

Athena nodded, her new pink hair swirling around her head like an enormous space helmet. "Geela has taken over the media networks, and she's trying to brainwash our people into thinking her dictatorship is a good thing. We want to encourage the residents of the planets of the Pentangle to fight back."

"The citizens of our galaxy have been living in peace for so long," Hera continued with a sigh. "But now that Geela has come in and taken over, we're worried about our planets beginning to fight among themselves. Someone has to remind the people of the Pentangle that staying unified in love and harmony will be better for everyone!"

"And also, we want to fight," Juno added. "To take Geela down."

Rhea flashed a charming smile at Chamberlin and said, "You have to admit . . . our rock star makeovers are fab, yeah? We totally look the part." She waved a hand in front of each of the other girls, urging Chamberlin to admire their new looks once again. "You must be happy we all look really different than we did yesterday! Operation: Disguise Princesses was a full-on success."

Chamberlin held a hand over his eyes. "I forbid you to form a band," he said quietly. He peeked at the girls through his fingers. They all smiled back at him, saying nothing. "You're not going to take no for an answer, are you?"

"Not a chance," Rhea said.

"Nope," agreed Juno.

"No offense, Chambermaid . . ." Luna said with a smile. "But you're totally out of your league here. It's five against one, and princesses always get what they want."

"Be a part of the solution, Chamberlin," Hera pleaded. "You're either with us . . . or against freedom."

Chamberlin groaned.

Athena strode across the kitchen, put her hands on Chamberlin's shoulders, and looked him in the eye. She pleaded, "Help us fix this, Chamberlin. The sooner we overthrow Geela, the sooner we all get to go home. Don't you miss the comforts of Athenia?"

Chamberlin shook his head. "I was given very specific orders to keep you here, out of harm's way. Your parents— and Rhea's royal protectors—put me in charge," he muttered. "Why do I suddenly feel like it's the other way around?" He shuffled out of the kitchen. A moment later, the girls heard his bedroom door swoosh closed.

"That went well," Rhea said, grinning at the others. "I think he'll come around."

"I think we'd have an easier time convincing him that this band is a good idea if we actually *sounded* like a band," Athena said matter-of-factly. "Let's write a song and show him we're serious."

Leaving the rest of their dishes on the table (the girls' pets had grown fond of cleaning leftovers off the dirty plates after every meal), SPACEPOP retreated to their common room. Athena sat primly in front of her keyboard, Rhea flopped onto her bed with the guitar resting on her belly, Hera stood in a corner of the room hugging her bass, Juno settled in at the drum kit with a fierce look in her eyes, and Luna stood smiling in the center of them all.

"Where do we even start?" Rhea asked, plucking a few chords. "I've done plenty of composing on my own, but I'm not much of a songwriter."

Juno began pounding at the drums, taking out all her frustrations on the homemade instrument. "Let's just bash it out!" she screamed.

"Whoa," Athena said. "You're going to break something—relax, Juno."

"I made these drums out of recycled trash," Juno growled. "If they break, I'll fix them. I'm furious about what's happening, so why not use my emotions for musical inspiration? Isn't that the whole point of making music? To express yourself?" She looked around at the other girls, who all looked skeptical. "Let's all try to bang something out. It feels good to throw your anger out there. And I think once we let all our energy out into the room, something good will come to us. Seriously."

One by one, each of the princesses began to play. It was a mess of chords and angry screaming and pounding drum beats. At first, they just sounded like a mess of noise. But after a few minutes of insanity, the band members all began to calm down and listen to one another. Rhea and Hera moved to stand side by side. Athena and Juno slowed down and layered their sound on top of the others. Then Luna began to sing, *"We 'bout to start something big . . ."*

She trailed off. But the other girls nodded, urging her to continue. Luna's beautiful voice carried over the sound of the other instruments, clear and pure. *"Don't know where . . . as long as we get there."*

Rhea chimed in, layering on another line. *"We 'bout to start something huge . . ."*

"Right here, right now!" Juno screamed.

"Right here, right now!" the other girls echoed.

They all quieted down, grinning madly at each other. The collection of pets returned to the room, obviously curious about what was happening. "That sounded pretty good," Hera cheered.

"It really did," Athena agreed. "Should we try it again, from the top? Let's all sing the last line together, okay?"

They began to play again. Luna sang: *"We 'bout to*

start something big . . . Don't know where, as long as we get there." She nodded at Rhea, who sang the next line. "*We 'bout to start something huge . . .*"

They all sang out, "*Right here, right now!*"

Then Athena dropped in the next line: "*We 'bout to start something new! Something you can't put in a . . .*" She paused, frowning.

"Box?" Hera suggested.

"*We 'bout to start something new . . . something you can't put in a box!*" Athena sang, laughing.

"*We 'bout to start something real!*" Rhea went on.

Juno yelled, "*Can't stop, won't stop!*" She waved her drumstick in the air and cried out, "Everyone, sing that line with me!"

They repeated the verse again, trying the last line together again. It was long past midnight when they finally had a complete draft of their first song. Each of the girls collapsed onto their beds, exhausted. Athena quickly grabbed a pen and an empty notebook and wrote down the full song so they wouldn't forget it:

[[Refrain]]
We 'bout to start something new
Don't know where, as long as we get there!
We 'bout to start something huge
Right here, right now!

We 'bout to start something new
Something you can't put in a box!
We 'bout to start something real
Can't stop, won't stop!
[[Verse One]]
Wishing on a shooting star, isn't gonna get you far
There's so much we gotta do . . . stick together, see it through
Why be just an average girl? . . . You can go and change the world
Right here, right now!
[[Refrain]]
[[Verse Two]]
Though the journey may be long . . . learning what is right or wrong
We just wanna sing our song . . . with each other we are strong
Why be just an average girl? . . . You can go and change the world!
Right here, right now! Can't stop, won't stop!
We 'bout to start something big!

"I think we have our first song," Athena said, looking up.

"How about we call it 'We 'Bout to Start Something Big'?" Luna suggested. There were murmurs of agreement from each of the other girls.

"I think," Chamberlin said, stepping into the girls' bedroom, "that song fits your situation nicely." He smiled. "I've been listening to your rehearsal tonight. Though I think this rock band silliness is a terrible plan and goes against absolutely everything I've been instructed to do, I must say: you sound rather lovely together."

"Really?" Juno said, smiling. "That's quite a compliment, coming from an old-school guy like you."

The curmudgeonly butler sighed, then went on, "While you were practicing tonight, I did a bit of research to see what this little rock band project of yours would entail. If you really are serious about pursuing it, we have quite a lot we'll need to do—to travel, we would need to turn our transport into a stylish tour bus. Then there's the matter of designing a band logo, finishing your costumes to ensure you're properly disguised . . ."

"I'm on that!" Rhea said. "Costumes will be done tomorrow, I think. There are just a few finishing touches to do on each one, but they're looking good. Right, girls?" The other four girls nodded. Rhea really had a knack for fashion design.

"I can handle the band logo," Juno chimed in. She shrugged and added, "I love graphic design and art. Never get much time to fiddle around with my art back home, but I'd love to give it a shot." The others gaped at her. "What?" Juno demanded.

Athena smiled reassuringly. "Nothing. We'd love for you to design our logo, Juno."

Chamberlin shook his head, clearly overwhelmed by how much there was to do, and how little control he had over the girls. "It also seems I may need to hire something called a roadie to help with some of the heavy lifting if and when we go out on tour. There is a qualified candidate—a chap by the name of Rand—here on Borana that we could talk to. I'm certainly too old for this nonsense, and I doubt very much that you girls will be willing to haul your own gear. We can make a bedroom for him in one of the storage closets, if need be."

"A *roadie*?" Luna cried. "You'd hire a roadie for us?"

"Chamberlin, you're the best!" Rhea said. "You know, I heard you say, '*when* we go out on tour . . .' You love this band idea, don't you? We're totally doing it!"

"We knew you'd come around," Juno said, winking.

"Thank you for supporting us, Chamberlin," Athena added.

"Now, now," Chamberlin said, waving his hand. "Let's not get ahead of ourselves. We'll see if we can make it work. But it will take a lot of preparation, hard work, and planning."

Before he could say anything more, Hera put her hands in the air and declared, "Let's celebrate the creation of our beautiful and inspiring new band . . . with a group hug!"

Laughing, the girls raced over and surrounded Chamberlin. The butler coughed in protest. "Oof!" he groaned, pushing them away. "Hands off your butler! If you squeeze me to death, someone else will have to drive this bus!"

CHAPTER SIX

AS THE SPACEPOP TOUR BUS BLASTED THROUGH THE PENTANGLE GALAXY, THE BAND PREPARED FOR ITS FIRST GIG ON LUNA'S HOME PLANET OF LUNARIA.

WE ARE TOTALLY GOING TO ROCK TONIGHT!

I'M SURE A TON OF LUNARIANS WILL COME OUT TO HEAR ME SING!

NEWS FLASH, LUNA: NO ONE KNOWS IT'S YOU. YOU'RE DISGUISED AS THE UNKNOWN LEAD SINGER OF A NEW BAND—REMEMBER?

THE SHOW IS GOING TO BE GREAT!

WHOA! THESE SHOES ARE HIGH!

ARE YOU **SURE** I CAN'T GO OUT ON STAGE IN BARE FEET?

EW! THAT IS **DISGUSTING**.

WE HAVE TO LOOK AND SOUND LIKE ROCK STARS TONIGHT!

THIS IS THE FIRST TIME ANYONE IN THE GALAXY IS GOING TO HEAR US. YOU NEVER GET A SECOND CHANCE AT A FIRST IMPRESSION.

OKAY! I'LL KEEP PRACTICING.

OOPSIE!

THEY LANDED ON LUNARIA...

EVERYTHING HAS CHANGED SO MUCH SINCE I LEFT...

OH MY GROCK!

GEELA DESTROYED THE SCULPTURE OF MY PARENTS AND ME!

I'M SO SORRY, LUNA.

GEELA IS SUCH A MEANIE!

THAT'S TERRIBLE.

WE HAVE TO TAKE THIS ANGER AND CHANNEL IT INTO OUR SHOW TONIGHT.

YEAH...I GUESS YOU'RE RIGHT. OKAY, GIRLS. I'M READY TO START SOMETHING BIG!

RAND—THE NEW ROADIE—IS WORKING OUT PRETTY WELL.

HE'S CLUMSY, BUT AT LEAST **I** DON'T HAVE TO CARRY ANYTHING.

THIS ISN'T **EXACTLY** WHAT I WAS EXPECTING.

I THOUGHT YOU SAID IT WAS A SUPER HOT PLACE?

IT **IS** HOT. THE CLUB'S WEBSITE SAID THEY KEEP THE TEMPERATURE AT 85 DEGREES.

WHAT'S WITH HE GAS MASKS?

THEY'RE **OXYGEN** MASKS. THE AIR BAR SERVES SCENTED OXYGEN—IT'S SUPPOSED TO BE AMAZING FOR YOUR SKIN.

THIS PLACE IS TOTALLY DEAD!

I THINK THIS GUY MIGHT ACTUALLY **BE** DEAD...

WE GO ON IN TEN MINUTES. EVEN IF THE CROWD IS FAST ASLEEP, THE SHOW MUST GO ON.

93

ONE, TWO, **ONE TWO THREE FOUR!**

♪ WE 'BOUT TO START SOMETHING NEW! DON'T KNOW WHERE, AS LONG AS WE GET THERE! WE 'BOUT TO START SOMETHING HUGE RIGHT HERE, RIGHT NOW! ♫

BUT AFTER A FEW MINUTES, THINGS BEGAN TO FALL APART.

CRIPPLED BY STAGE FRIGHT, RHEA FORGOT EVERY SINGLE ONE OF HER LYRICS . . .

♪ BLAH, BLAH, SOMETHING ABOUT . . . SOMETHING? ♪

RAND FORGOT TO CONNECT ATHENA'S KEYBOARD TO THE SOUND SYSTEM, SO NO ONE COULD HEAR HER.

PLINK
PLINK
PLINK

HERA KEPT FALLING OVER IN HER NEW SHOES . . .

OOF!

JUNO HAD SOME TROUBLE KEEPING HER ANGER IN CHECK . . .

WAKE UP, SLEEPING BEAUTY!

AND LUNA SPENT THE WHOLE SECOND HALF OF THE CONCERT CRYING.

WHERE ARE ALL MY **FANS**?

SOB!

BY THE TIME THE GIRLS TOOK THEIR FINAL BOWS, EVERYONE WAS EAGER TO GET OFF LUNARIA.

IT'S OKAY, LUNA . . .

SMELLS SO FRESH AND FRAGRANCE-FREE OUT HERE! THE AIR BAR STINKS!

NO ONE SHOWED UP! NO ONE CHEERED! NO ONE WANTED MY AUTOGRAPH!

SOB!

DID YOU THINK WE WOULD BECOME INSTANT ROCK STARS?

OF COURSE THAT'S WHAT I EXPECTED. HOW DARE MY PEOPLE NOT SHOW UP TO SUPPORT MY FIRST GIG?

NO ONE KNOWS IT WAS YOU PLAYING HERE TONIGHT. IF ANYONE HAD REALIZED IT WAS THE ROYAL PRINCESS PLAYING ON STAGE, I'M SURE THE PLACE WOULD HAVE BEEN PACKED.

OH MY GROCK . . .

OH MY GROCK . . .

OH MY GROCK . . . IT'S YOU!

OUR COVER IS BLOWN ALREADY?

YOU KNOW WHO WE ARE?

OF **COURSE** I KNOW WHO YOU ARE! YOU'RE SPACEPOP! YOU JUST PLAYED, RIGHT?

YES, **WE ARE** SPACEPOP! DID YOU LIKE OUR SET?

LIKE IT? I **LOVED** IT! I'M BRADBURY. AND AS OF THIS MOMENT, I'M YOUR NUMBER-ONE FAN.

FAN? WEREN'T YOU THE DUDE NAPPING IN THE BACK OF THE ROOM?

NOT NAPPING . . . SOAKING IT ALL IN! YOU WERE INCREDIBLE. YOUR SONGS ARE INSPIRING, YOUR SOUND IS FRESH, AND YOU'RE ALL—YOU'RE ALL SO PRETTY!

AND FIERCE!

IT WASN'T THE BEST FIRST GIG . . . BUT AT LEAST SPACEPOP HAD ALREADY FOUND ITS BIGGEST FAN!

I CAN'T WAIT TO TELL EVERYONE ABOUT SPACEPOP! I'LL MAKE SURE EVERYONE IN THE GALAXY HEARS YOUR SONG. YOU ARE GOING TO BE HUGE STARS. LIKE, *ROYALTY* HUGE. FAMOUS!

THANK YOU, BRADBURY!

YOU ARE AMAZING, BRADBURY. IT'S ALWAYS WONDERFUL TO FIND SOMEONE WHO WORSHIPS ME!

CHAPTER 7

"SO HOW LONG HAVE YOU KNOWN CHAMBERLIN?" Rhea asked Athena as the SPACEPOP tour bus raced through space a few weeks after Geela's takeover. The two girls had been trying to write a new song for several hours, but they weren't getting very far. Luna was the most talented songwriter in the group, but she always kept the best lines for herself. Chamberlin had set their space bus coordinates for Hera's home planet, Heralda, where the band's next gig was scheduled. Hera was in the middle of the living room meditating with Roxie, Juno and Skitter were both working out, and Luna and Adora were happily napping.

"Chamberlin has been in my family's service since long before I was born," Athena said. Beside her, Mykie nodded along. "He's a member of an ancient Felian race, born and bred to serve at the highest levels."

"So instead of being born into royalty, Chamberlin was born into service?" Rhea asked. On the floor, Springle clumsily fiddled with the strings of Rhea's guitar while Rhea took a break.

"Yes," Athena said. "He is extremely good at his job. He's a bit old school, but it's appropriate given his position."

"I wonder if he ever resents it," Rhea said. "Being forced to take care of others, instead of being allowed to choose his path?"

"I asked him that once, when I was little and didn't realize it was inappropriate for a princess to ask such questions," Athena said. "He told me he would much rather have *his* job than mine. He enjoys tending to others' needs. And he believes our royal obligations are far more challenging than his duties." Athena smiled. "I must say I agree with him—living on our own without our usual tasks has been quite nice. I certainly would have liked to have more servants around to help with painting our logo on the space bus, but some freedom from our usual duties has been refreshing." She nodded to Rhea. "Do you ever wonder what your life would be like if you hadn't been born into royalty?"

"All the time!" Rhea said. "Because I *wasn't* born into royalty. For a long time I lived a really different life. You know they didn't discover I was a princess until I was five, right? I was living in an orphanage. I was moved to the palace after they discovered I have royal blood."

"I heard that," Athena said. "It must have been interesting living such a simple existence for a time. What was it like?"

Rhea shrugged. "I don't remember much about my toddler years. But after all those years of having nothing—no servants, too little food, only one change of clothes—I certainly appreciate all of the privileges I have now." She picked up her guitar, strummed a few out-of-tune notes, then went on, "The one thing I missed after I left the orphanage was affection. The nurses were very sweet to all of the other children and me. Once I was removed from their care and brought to the palace, I felt very alone much of the time. It's been nice being here with all of you. It's the first time I've felt like I have a real family." She grinned. "I realize that sounds silly."

Athena shook her head. "It doesn't sound silly." She and Rhea smiled at each other.

A moment later, Hera skipped into the room.

"Chamberlin just told me we've entered the Heralda atmosphere." She snuggled her pet close in her arms and cooed, "Aren't you just so excited to visit home, Roxie? Aren't you?"

Luna poked her head out of her sleeping pod, her eyes barely open. "Are we there?" Luna whispered. "Am I on? Where's my juice?"

"We'll be there soon," Rhea told her. "We should be landing in a few minutes. You probably ought to start your beauty regimen now. The show starts in less than four hours."

Luna looked panicked. "Why didn't someone wake me sooner? You *know* it takes at least two hours to perfect my makeup, I need an hour to warm up my voice, and I haven't even decided what I'm going to wear yet." She stared wildly around the room. "Isn't anyone going to lay out my outfit?!"

Rhea glanced at Athena and muttered, "I might take back what I said about enjoying living with all of you. There was a lot less drama when I lived alone."

When the SPACEPOP tour bus landed on Heralda and the girls stepped outside, the destruction from Geela's takeover was immediately obvious. Their transport was parked on a charred brown field. As far as they could see, Heralda was nothing but a dead wasteland. The sky was smoky and brown, and the only sound was the droning buzz of one of Geela's Android ships flying overhead. Hera had been telling the other girls about her planet for days, bragging about endless fields of flowers, the lush, green prairies, and relaxing birdsong that filled her planet with hope and happiness. Now, all that was gone.

Hera scanned the horizon, her always-hopeful expression morphing into devastation as she realized what had become of her beautiful planet under Geela's brief reign. Suddenly, Hera took off at a run. The girls raced after her as she ran from their ship. They all scrambled up a mossy hill, then came to a stop on a rocky overlook. Below them, more burned fields and a pile of rubble littered a narrow valley. It was obvious they were looking at the scattered remains of Hera's former home. The elegant castle was nothing more than a pile of broken stones and colored glass.

"I'm so sorry," Luna said, wrapping her arm tenderly around Hera's shoulders. Hera dropped her head onto Luna's shoulder.

The other three girls moved in around them, holding Hera up as she broke down and wept—for her home, her planet, and her people. "It's all gone," she sobbed. "The flowers, my animal shrubs, the fairy gardens, the birds . . . everything. It's gone!"

There was nothing the others could say to make it

better. The reality was, Geela had destroyed everything Hera held dear. The evil empress had taken Hera's parents prisoner, destroyed a beautiful planet, and delivered fear and terror to the people of Heralda. While the other princesses of the Pentangle tried to comfort Hera, they couldn't stop themselves from wondering if other planets had succumbed to a similar fate. Had Geela destroyed the entire galaxy? And for what? To exert her power?

"I spent my whole life nurturing and growing the gardens at the back of the castle," Hera said quietly.

"Don't worry, Hera," Athena said. "Someday, we will rebuild our palaces, our planets, and our lives."

Hera took a deep breath and announced, "You're right. Geela may have started this fight . . . but we're going to end it. That evil beast has no idea who she's dealing with."

☆　☆　☆　☆　☆

"One . . . two . . . *one two three four*!" Juno screamed into her microphone, kicking off the last song of the SPACEPOP set a few hours later. The band had been rocking out on a spinning stage in the center of a small island on Heralda for nearly forty-five minutes. They were far enough from Hera's family castle and the capital that Geela hadn't yet had a chance to destroy the festival grounds. Fluffy trees and fairy gardens sur-rounded the stage, and the air smelled like cinnamon and clover. Now that they had seen how beautiful Heralda was, the other girls could truly understand the extent of the devastation near Hera's home.

SPACEPOP was one of several bands that had been given a slot to perform during a weekend art festival. The crowd was small—and no one was really there for the music—but those who had stopped to listen to them play were energetic and seemed to be totally engrossed in SPACEPOP's sound. A few of them even sang along, which thrilled Luna beyond measure.

At one point during their set, Rhea leaned in to asked Hera, "How do they know our lyrics?"

"No clue," Hera shrugged. "But I love it!"

After witnessing Geela's brutal destruction on Heralda that afternoon, the band had managed to channel their anger into a powerful performance. The lyrics of "We 'Bout to Start Something Big" felt more important than ever. Their mission was more urgent, and that intensity was reflected in their set.

As they wrapped up their final song, Luna looked at her bandmates and sang out, *"Why be just an average girl? . . . You can go and change the world!"*

Hera and the others chimed in, *"Right here, right now! Can't stop, won't stop!"*

When they wrapped their set, SPACEPOP took a bow and grinned at one another. "That was amazing! I rocked!" Luna gushed. "I mean . . . *we* rocked."

An eager fan rushed the stage and cried, "You *did* rock! Luna, I love you!"

For a moment, Luna looked taken aback. In her life as a princess, she wasn't accustomed to being approached by fans and commoners. Every interaction with the public was carefully scripted and arranged to ensure that she wouldn't ever come into contact with germs or smelly people. But in the next moment, Luna seemed to remember she was a budding rock star, and instead of stepping back, she splashed a charming smile across her face and said, "Oh, wow. Thanks so much!"

"Can I have your autograph?" the fan begged. "I'll pay you for it!" The girl rustled around in her bag, holding up a wrinkled note. "This is all I have—is it enough?"

Luna waved her hand in the air. "Don't be silly. Of *course* I'll give you an autograph. No need to pay."

"Oh my Grock," the young girl said, fanning herself. "Bradbury said you were nice. But I didn't realize you would be *this* nice!"

"Bradbury?" Athena asked as Luna scrawled her loopy signature on the back of their newest fan's shirt.

"You know . . . your biggest fan," the girl said. "You

met him on Lunaria? He's been talking about you non-stop since your Air Bar show."

"Really?" Rhea said, lifting an eyebrow.

The girl nodded earnestly. "Really. He told all of us to come today. He was super sad he had to work and miss it. He said you're the next big thing."

The girls exchanged a baffled look. "So, this Bradbury has a . . . following?" Athena asked finally.

"You don't *know* about Bradbury?" the girl said, her single eye widening. "He is, like, the king of fan vlogs. He started one about you right after your show at Air Bar. I hope this doesn't get him in trouble, but he even posted all the lyrics to "We 'Bout to Start Something Big" in his first vlog. My friends and I totally worship you! We've been dying to see you live. We all absolutely love your message." The girl suddenly gasped and said, "Please *please please please* can I interview you for my blog? I only have sixty-four followers, but they're really good followers!"

"Um," Rhea said. "Sure?"

"Yay!" the girl cheered. Then she dug around in her bag again, searching for something. "Oh my Grock, this is so embarrassing. So, I don't have my stuff with me right now, but if I'm at your next gig, can I interview you then?"

"Of course," Hera said, leaning in to give her a hug.

"I love you, SPACEPOP!" the girl said, backing away. "Love! You!"

"Well," Athena said, as soon as she was gone. "That went well."

"We should really buy that Bradbury guy some choco-lates or something," Rhea said. "It seems like it might not be a bad idea to stay on his good side."

As they made their way out of the festival, heading back to the tour bus to meet up with Chamberlin (who had returned to the bus to make a few necessary repairs while the girls signed autographs), the girls came upon a courtyard plastered with Geela propaganda posters. The so-called empress's cold face stared back at them from every available surface. Posters were hanging from lan-terns and shrubs and potted plants, and they littered the mosaic-tiled ground.

"This courtyard used to be filled with flowers and com-munity yoga mats," Hera said, looking around sadly. "It was a gathering place for the people of Heralda to recharge and relax."

"It's not very relaxing now," Athena said.

"It's downright creepy with Geela staring at us," Hera shivered. "It feels like she's here, watching our every move."

Juno stepped up to one of the posters and sneered at Geela's picture. "You can't defeat us!" she hissed. "We will fight back. Just watch what SPACEPOP is going to do."

On the other side of the courtyard, Rhea suddenly began to giggle. "What do you girls think? Doesn't she look better this way?" she whispered. She stepped back, revealing the mustache and glasses she had drawn on the poster of Geela.

"Rhea!" Luna gasped, glancing around nervously. They were totally alone, but Hera was right: it felt like they were being watched. "You can't do that!"

"I can," Rhea said. "And I will." She took a marker and began decorating another poster—drawing little spikes and a goatee on the empress's face. After only a moment's hesitation, Hera and Juno joined her. They laughed and scribbled, filling the posters with graffiti.

Athena and Luna exchanged nervous looks. "This is very childish," Athena said.

"And we're going to get in so much trouble if someone catches us!" Luna pointed out.

"Have some fun," Rhea urged, making dots all over Geela's face on another poster. "Trust me when I say it feels *really* good." She handed Athena a marker and pushed her toward one of the posters. "Live a little." Then she grinned at Luna and said, "You know you want to."

Athena sighed. Timidly, she drew a huge, clownish frown on one of the posters—then began to laugh. In no time, every single one of the posters had been defaced, and all five of the girls felt a lot better. It was a tiny victory, a silly thing, but the act of making Geela look like a fool had helped to make the girls feel like they had gotten a little bit of revenge for what she'd done to Hera's and Luna's homes.

The princesses of POP high-fived each other, then raced away from the courtyard. But as they ran down a long tree-lined pathway to their tour bus, a dark figure stepped out of the shadows. "I saw what you just did," the figure said in a low, growling voice. "And now I think the five of you need to come with me."

PART THREE: **BAND TOGETHER**

CHAPTER 8

JUNO PUT UP HER FISTS AND PREPARED TO FIGHT. "Run!" she told the other girls. "Get to the bus—tell Chamberlin we need to hit the space road *now*!"

"We're not leaving you," Athena told her. "We're in this together. We will all take responsibility for what we've done."

The dark figure chuckled. "Well, well, that certainly is a noble statement," he said. The man—who was green-skinned with multi-colored hair shaved into a Mohawk across the top of his head—stepped out of the shadows, smiling broadly at them. "I'm not here to punish you. I'm here with a proposition."

Four of the princesses eyed him suspiciously. Luna,

however, swooned. The young alien was incredibly cute, and she was obviously *very* distracted by his good looks. Like every good hero, this guy was wearing a beret, he was clearly very strong and muscular, and the stubble on his chin? Totally flirty. Luna was hooked. And judging by the way she was ogling him, the man probably could have told them he was taking them to a dark prison and she would have willingly joined him.

"Do you know who I am?" the man asked.

"No," Juno said defiantly. "Are you one of Geela's ugly henchmen?"

"Ugly?" Luna said, giggling nervously. "That's so *mean*, Juno!"

The man chuckled again. "I . . . am Captain Hansome." He said this with a flourish, as though his name should have inspired worship and cheers.

"What do you want from us?" Athena asked.

"Are we in some kind of trouble?" Hera said nervously.

"We cannot discuss it here," Captain Hansome said, retreating into the shadows again. "I need you to come with me. There is much for us to discuss, but it is dangerous to be meeting like this out in the open. Walk with me."

"You want us to *walk* with you?" Rhea scoffed. "You seriously want five girls to follow some guy they just met to some unknown location? Do you think we're *stupid*?"

Hansome sighed. "I see your point." He seemed to consider his options for a moment, then slipped under the drooping branches of a nearby willow tree. "*Pssst*," he hissed. "In here!"

The five princesses exchanged wary looks. Rhea shook her head. "This guy is classic," she said. "I have to admit, I'm a little curious."

"What could he possibly want from us?" Athena wondered.

"Only one way to find out," Juno said, then slipped between the tree's hanging branches.

Once they were all gathered under the tree's canopy, Captain Hansome smiled broadly. "Ah, yes, welcome. And thank you all for meeting with me tonight."

Rhea snorted. "Can you just get to the point? Why did you stop us?"

"I have heard your music," Hansome said solemnly.

"Oh!" Luna said brightly. "Are you a fan?"

"No," Hansome said. "I am not."

"Oh," Luna said, sniffing. "Well, why not?"

Hansome took a deep, serious breath and said, "Let me ask you this: Have you heard . . . of the *Resistance*?"

"Is that a band or something?" Hera wondered.

"No, I am not speaking of a band," Hansome said, obviously offended. "I am talking about . . . the *Resistance*!"

"Do you have to say it like that?" Rhea asked, giggling. "With that dramatic pause before you say . . . 'the *Resistance*'?"

"Do you want to join, or not?" Hansome asked impatiently.

"Join what?" Luna asked in a moony voice. "If there's something you want me to join, I totally will!"

"Luna!" Athena scolded. "You can't agree to join something when you don't even know what you're joining!"

"What is . . . the *Resistance*?" Juno asked, imitating Hansome's ridiculous tone.

"We are a group of freedom fighters," Captain Hansome said, puffing out his chest. "A secret group of rebels, working against Geela. We call ourselves . . . the *Resistance*."

"Yeah," Rhea snickered. "We got that."

"We have heard some of your songs—and I saw what you did to Geela's posters back there in the courtyard," Hansome said. "I think you would be a good addition to our team. No one would expect a bunch of singers to be part of a larger mission to overthrow Geela."

"Oh, pal," Rhea said under her breath. "You have *no* idea."

"So what do you say?" Hansome asked seriously. "Are you in . . . or *are you out*?"

"Hold on," Athena said. The princess of Athenia had

been raised to be cautious. She wasn't about to agree to some sort of rebel mission without being sure of whom she was dealing with. "How do we know we can trust you? How do we know you're not actually working for Geela? Maybe she's sent you off on a mission to hunt down all the citizens of the Pentangle who don't like her, and this is some kind of trap."

"Huh," Hansome said. "That is also a good point. But! How do I know *I* can trust you? We are in a similar predicament, you see. You are strangers to me, I am a stranger to you."

"Let's not be strangers," Luna said, her voice soft and flirty.

"Ugh," Juno said, nudging her. "Say we *do* decide to trust you, Hansome. What happens next? Do we just say, 'yeah, sure, we'll join . . . the *Resistance*, and all is well? Or do you want us to actually do something for you to prove ourselves?"

"Prove yourselves," Hansome said, running a hand across his chin. "Yes, yes that is an excellent plan. I have a small mission for you. A test, if you will. If you are successful, there will be more. So what do you say? Are you willing to be a part of . . . the *Resistance*?"

"Absolutely!" Luna said, nodding. She looked at the other girls in the tree-covered shadows. "Right, girls? We're in, aren't we?"

"What is it you have in mind?" Athena asked reasonably.

Hansome leaned in closer to the five girls and said in a hushed whisper, "In the remote Ice Desert on Heralda, we have received reports that Geela is building a new weapon. I need a team to scout and report what kind of weapon she is building." He paused for dramatic emphasis. "With this information, we will be able to determine the best way to destroy it."

"That's the mission?" Juno asked. "You just want us to find it and tell you what we've found? We don't actually get to destroy it ourselves?"

"Absolutely not!" Hansome said, laughing. "Leave that to the experts. You are merely trainees. If you impress me, you *may* have the opportunity to do something bigger. But for now, don't do anything dangerous. The *Resistance* doesn't want to be responsible for any unplanned casualties."

"We're on it," Rhea said. "And *if* we like the mission, maybe we'll be willing to do more for . . . the *Resistance*." She smiled. "Let's just consider this a test run on *both* sides, shall we?"

"Indeed," Hansome replied. "I will send a supply pod with a few things that might be of use to you on the mission, as well as general directions to the Ice Desert."

"What if we have questions?" Luna said, batting her eyelashes. "Should I call you?"

Hansome shook his head firmly. "I will be in contact with you. All messages and communications will be encrypted and protected with security measures. In order to unlock and listen to our correspondence, you'll all need to be present. My team collected your fingerprints from your equipment earlier today—"

Rhea cut him off. "They did *what* now?"

"They lifted your prints from the microphones . . ." Hansome said casually. "And from your drumsticks, Juno. It's very easy to do."

"How dare you take our prints without permission!" Athena growled.

"Geela has done far worse without anyone's permission," Hansome reminded them. "Now. As I was saying, each of you will need to be present in order to receive my communications. Five sets of prints. Understood?" He scanned their faces, and each girl nodded her agreement.

Suddenly, Athena thought of Chamberlin and how he would react to their new assignment. She had a feeling he would probably insist that he join them, in order to fulfill his orders to protect the princesses at all costs. "What about our . . . *manager*?" she asked. "Chamberlin. He will, of course, be joining us on these missions."

"Seriously?" Captain Hansome muttered.

"Yes," Rhea agreed. "He's very involved. Hands-on and all that."

"Fine," Hansome groaned. "Honestly, you rock stars and your babysitters. It's ridiculous." He took a deep breath and added, "Wait for my orders. Be ready." He waved his hand in the air, then slipped between two branches and disappeared.

As soon as he was gone, Juno grumbled, "I don't like the way that guy underestimates us. You know what I think? I think we need to show *Captain* Hansome what five angry teenage girls are capable of. Because the five of us . . . we are *not* your average princesses."

CHAPTER 9

"YOU DID *WHAT*?" CHAMBERLIN SCREECHED. "YOU met with *whom*?"

"Captain Hansome," Athena explained, for the sixth time. "He intercepted us as we returned to the transport tonight. He's asked us to help with"—she lowered her voice—"the *Resistance*."

Chamberlin paced back and forth in the living room of their tour bus, obviously agitated. "How *could* you, Athena?"

"Why *not*, Chamberlin?" she snapped back. "The whole point of us forming this band is to spread the rebel message. Why not help in more obvious ways, too?"

"Because you could get hurt, that's why!" Chamberlin

said, his voice trembling. "Oh my, oh my, oh my . . . this is an absolute disaster. First a band, now rebel activities. What's next? Shooting at Geela's ship with a bow and arrow?"

"That's more Juno's style," Athena said. "I recognize that hand-to-hand combat is silly in a situation like this. Geela has many protectors and is not likely to be vulnerable to a physical attack."

"I wasn't being serious!" Chamberlin gasped. He stormed into the hangout area, where the other girls were waiting for Athena to help them write a new song. After the day's excitement, everyone was in the mood to create. They all felt inspired to write their next song as they prepared for their first rebel mission. "All of you!" Chamberlin barked, shaking his finger at the five girls. "You are being careless and reckless. This is *not* part of our agreement! When I agreed to help the five of you disguise yourselves as—"

Chamberlin paused as Rand came strolling through, carrying a pizza in one hand and a video game console in the other. The five girls and Chamberlin stared at their roadie, waiting for him to move on through. They had to be careful not to talk about rebel activity, their true identities, or their home planets whenever Rand was around. As far as he was concerned, he was simply working for a brand-new band.

"Uh, hiya?" Rand said through a mouthful of pizza. "My shift is done for tonight, right?"

"Absolutely, Rand," Chamberlin said firmly. "You are dismissed."

Rand could clearly sense that he had walked into the middle of something. He looked at the girls sheepishly, then held out his pizza and said, "Does anyone want a bite?" They all shook their heads no. "All righty then. I'm gonna crash."

Whistling, he strolled out of the room and let the girls and Chamberlin get on with their discussion.

"As I was saying—" Chamberlin began again.

But Juno cut him off. "Yeah, yeah, you don't support us working with Captain Hansome. That's totally expected."

"Yet you're doing it *anyway*?" Chamberlin said, aghast.

"Obviously," Luna shrugged. "For one thing, he's super cute and dresses well."

"And for another, he's helping us actually do something to fight back against Geela," Rhea explained. "Performing our music is great, but it feels good to have something concrete to do that will threaten her power more quickly."

"And he asked nicely," Hera said, nodding.

Chamberlin sat on the edge of the sofa, resting his face in his hands. "He asked nicely?" he muttered. "So you're going to join a rebel army because someone *asked nicely?*" Chamberlin's shoulders dropped. "Honestly, how do I get into these things? What have I done to deserve this job? Did *anyone* in any of the royal courts honestly believe I could succeed in this mission?"

"Don't beat yourself up, Chamberlin," Juno said, patting him on the back. "No one is going to stop any of us once we've decided to do something."

"We're princesses," Luna said. "We get what we want and need. Eventually, we'll get rid of Geela—it's just a matter of time."

"Where there's a will," Hera chirped. "There's a way!"

The next afternoon, before setting out on their first mission for the Resistance, SPACEPOP decided to test out some of its new material in a park on Heralda. "My people seem really down," Hera had said the night before. "I'd love to play for everyone, to help bring a little light to the darkness on our planet."

So the next morning, the girls enlisted Rand to set up their equipment near a children's play area in a busy central park. Heralda had been filled with parks and gardens—and now those that hadn't yet been destroyed by Geela were filled with people out enjoying what remained of their planet's natural beauty—but Hera had been specific about where she wanted to play.

"I want to go to Trueberry Meadow. It was my favorite park to play in when I was a little kid," she explained. "When I was small, my parents thought it would benefit me to mingle with the people of our planet. They used to have nannies take me to the park to run and frolic with some of the other children of Heralda."

"That's so different from my upbringing," Athena said distantly.

"Same," Luna said. "I was carefully shielded from the outside world. For my own protection, of course."

"It was really nice to get to play with other kids for a while," Hera said. Then she frowned. "But when I turned eight, I was expected to begin my formal princess training. So there was no longer time for me to go to the park with all the other children. Of course, I was still encouraged to play outside with my nannies and tutors and the servants around the castle, but I so missed being around kids my own age. I've always cherished the fond memories I have from the days I spent at that park. I had photographs of the park hanging over my bed back home. They brought me much joy when I woke each morning," she said wistfully. "So now, I'd love to share our message of joy, peace, and love at Trueberry Meadow—as a way of giving back."

"Well, let's get out there and spread some cheer," Juno said, grabbing her drumsticks. "Because we have a mission to accomplish, and I have no intention of failing."

A short while later, Rand had the band's equipment set up on a huge rock in the center of Trueberry Meadow. They had to play acoustic, since there was nowhere to plug in amps or other sound equipment. Luckily, their location on top of the rounded rock helped the sound carry to the farthest edges of the park, and by the time they were on their second song, a sizable crowd had gathered.

"Look," Rhea said, nudging Athena between songs. "Isn't it that guy Bradbury?"

Sure enough, SPACEPOP's biggest fan was right up at the front of the crowd. He was bopping his head along with the music and capturing each of their songs on a tiny camera built into his glasses.

"I hope he likes the new song," Athena said, nodding curtly at Bradbury. "We can't afford to lose this guy's support."

Bradbury grinned and waved. Rhea waved back, then muttered to Athena, "Judging from the way he stares at Juno, I think we've found a forever-fan. I don't think we need to worry."

When the girls had reached the end of their usual set, Juno tapped out the beat of their newest song—"Have a

Good Time"—and Luna launched into the lyrics with backup from the other girls and their pets.

Turn up the music. . . . Turn down the drama.
Turn up the music. . . . Turn down the drama.
Yeah yeah yeah yea-aah. Yeah yeah yeah yeah eh ehh.
Yeah yeah yeah yea-aah. Yeah yeah yeah yeah eh ehh.
Yeah, we gonna have a good time. Yeah, we gonna have a good time.
Yeah, we gonna have a good time. Yeah, we gonna have a good time.
Our mission . . .
Gotta spread our message of friendship . . .
Through music, fashion, and freedom . . .
Yeah — don't forget the fun!
Remember . . . together there is no issue . . .
SPACEPOP is gonna be with you! SO . . .
Don't forget the fun!
Yeah yeah yeah yea-aah. Yeah yeah yeah yeah eh ehh.
Yeah yeah yeah yea-aah. Yeah yeah yeah yeah eh ehh.
Yeah, we gonna have a good time. Yeah, we gonna have a good time.
Yeah, we gonna have a good time. Yeah, we gonna have a good time.
Say-ay-ay-ay . . .

When they finished, the crowd went wild. People rushed forward to ask them for autographs, and dozens of new fans dropped tips into Rhea's guitar case. Luna soaked up

all the attention, while Hera tried to keep a low profile—
if any one of them were going to be recognized on
Heralda, it was Hera. Though she wanted to talk with
the people of her planet more than anything, to comfort
them and assure them that life would eventually go back
to normal, she knew she had to protect her cover. So she
just watched as Luna and Athena greeted their newest
fans. Juno went over to greet Bradbury. "Hey, Bradbury,"
she said. "Thanks for coming."

"I wouldn't miss this for anything," Bradbury gushed.
"It was almost impossible to get here in time—the
empress is trying to sort out all the galaxy's travel prob-
lems, you know—but the price of the private flight was
worth it for this. I'm your biggest fan."

"Have you met our manager, Chamberlin?" Rhea
asked, pushing Chamberlin forward to say hello.

"Oh, wow," Bradbury said breathlessly. "It's so good to
meet you, Mr. Chamberlin, sir." He reached out to shake
his hand.

Chamberlin bowed slightly and said, "Just Chamberlin,
please. I'm not *that* old."

While Juno and Chamberlin answered a few questions
for Bradbury's online fan vlog, Rhea dug through her
case to see what they had earned at their first paying gig.
Many people had given them money, a few had donated
space bus tokens, one person had put a sock in the case,

and there were two torn Geela posters. Rhea grinned when she saw the destroyed posters—their message was getting through to people! "Hey, Rand," she yelled, pulling out the last thing in her case. She tossed him a wrapped mooncheese sandwich. "Looks like you got a tip, buddy!"

"Yum! I love mooncheese sandwiches!" Rand cheered. "Thanks, Rhea."

Rhea shrugged. "Anytime."

As soon as the crowds in the park had dispersed, the SPACEPOP rebels slipped into the bus to change for their first mission for the Resistance. Hansome had sent the girls a package with their final instructions (a few less-than-helpful directions recorded on a self-destructing pod) and five black rebel outfits. In theory, the suits were supposed to make the girls less conspicuous—but outfitted in their matching black suits, the girls looked ultra-suspicious. "Really?" Juno said, surveying the other four girls in their coordinated rebel suits. "He thinks this is sneaky?"

"We look like cat burglars," Rhea said.

"Oh, I would never steal a cat!" Hera said, shaking her head seriously.

"That's not—" Rhea began. She sighed. "Nevermind."

"We've either got to wear these outfits, our SPACEPOP show costumes, or our princess clothes," Athena pointed out. "We don't have much of a choice."

"All right, then," Luna said, zipping her suit up under her chin. "Let's grab Chamberlin and go."

"I'm sorry . . . what?" Chamberlin said, poking his head into the girls' bedroom.

"Are you ready for our first rebel mission, Chamberlin?" Athena asked.

"Princess Athena," Chamberlin said in a low voice, "I was just consulting the Book of Grock about this mission . . ."

Juno raised her eyebrows at him.

Chamberlin opened a large, gilded book and began to read, "Grock said unto Beebopalula, if you go unto the Ice Desert, the royal butler shall stay behind and wait in a comfy chair and sip hot tea and then take a nap."

"Nice try, Chamberlin," Athena said. "But you promised our parents you'd watch out for us—remember? You took an oath."

"Your word," Rhea told him. "Not ours."

Chamberlin groaned. "Fine. But you must remember what Captain Hansome said: nothing dangerous. I need you all alive and unbroken for when the time comes to rule your planets again."

"We'll do what we must during this mission," Athena said firmly. "Because if we don't help overthrow Geela, we won't have any planets left to rule—ever."

CHAPTER 10

AS SOON AS THE SUN HAD SET ON THE PEACEFUL plane of Heralda, the girls and Chamberlin set off on their first mission for the Resistance. They made their way across a rocky field, then stopped.

Chamberlin huffed, "We can't possibly be *walking* to the Ice Desert?"

"Perhaps we should have taken the space bus," Rhea said, snapping her fingers. "No one would have guessed it was us. Oh, wait—our logo is painted across the side. That just *might* have been a giveaway."

"But the Ice Desert is . . . far!" Chamberlin whined.

Juno grinned. "Don't worry. I have a different idea." She whistled, then called out, "Skitter!"

Juno's little pet came scuttling out of the shadows. The furry little ball of muscle looked up at Juno expectantly. "Skitter!" she cooed. "Who's a big girl?"

Skitter grunted—*blurp!*—and began to grow.

Blurp! Blurp! Blurp!

With each loud *blurp!* the little creature grew bigger and bigger. Soon, she was five times her usual size.

She continued to grow until she was towering over them all. "Mount up!" Athena ordered. "This little beast will bounce us over."

The now enormous Skitter bent down and the girls climbed onto her back. "Whee!" Hera cried. "Giddy-up!"

Chamberlin looked skyward. "Why must everything be so complicated?!" He groaned, then reluctantly let Juno and Rhea help pull him up onto the mount. "Where are the seat belts?" he asked, digging around in Skitter's fur. "I refuse to let this thing blast off without a safety net of some kind!"

"You'll be fine. I've done this a hundred times." Juno tapped Skitter's head, then hollered, "Bounce away, Skitter!"

Fewer than twenty minutes later, the princesses and Chamberlin set down at the edge of the Ice Desert. Across a wide, icy plain, there was a large warehouse of some kind. It was all lit up, a beacon in the middle of the barren landscape. The girls hopped off their transport, and Skitter set about letting out some of his excess air.

Pffffft! Pffffft! Moments later, Juno's little pet was back to her normal size.

Juno gestured to the warehouse across the icy plain. On the edge of the stark white building, a giant red GEELA logo shone brightly. "So . . . our mission is to find Geela's secret warehouse and figure out what kind of weapon she's building?"

Rhea nodded. "Someone might want to let Geela know that putting her logo on the edge of a supposedly 'secret' warehouse isn't the best way to keep it a secret."

"The first part of the mission was easy," Athena said. "But the next part—sneaking inside and getting a look at what she's building—won't be as simple."

"Maybe someone should stay here and be the lookout?" Chamberlin suggested. "We could have some sort of sign, if I see any danger approaching!"

"Quit being such a worrywart, Chamberlin," Hera said, giggling. "I'm sure Geela isn't even *on* Heralda."

But as the girls and Chamberlin hustled across the icy landscape and drew closer to the warehouse, Geela's evil laugh echoed out around them.

"What is that?" Chamberlin asked, whimpering.

"I think it's Geela's laugh," Athena cringed. "Creepy. She must be nearby. So we'll need to be even more careful not to be seen."

"Thank Grock for our all-black outfits," Hera murmured.

"If it weren't for this clever disguise, I'm sure we'd have been spotted by now."

The girls and Chamberlin peeked around the side of the warehouse. There was a team of guards stationed in front of the doors. They were both outfitted with stun guns and full armor. "Looks like we have no way in," Chamberlin mused. "I guess we should turn back."

"I have an idea," Juno said. She whispered something into Skitter's ear. The little pet nodded once, then began to snort again. She ballooned up to the size of a large dog, then bounded past the guards back out into the Ice Desert.

"What was that?" one of them shrieked.

"Looked like a flying ball of fur!" the other answered.

"What are we supposed to do?" the first asked.

"Uh . . ." muttered the second. "I guess we should probably investigate?"

The two guards raced away from their post, trailing Skitter across the icy wasteland.

"Go!" Athena said. Moments later, the six of them were scrambling through the unguarded side door of the warehouse. They crouched low, trying not to be seen. The warehouse was one large room, with a maze of ducts and passageways crisscrossing overhead. There were machines everywhere, churning and buzzing and clacking as they created new weapons for Geela.

"Will Skitter be okay?" Hera asked, glancing nervously back at the door they had entered from. "I feel just awful leaving her out there with those two horrible guards."

"She'll be fine," Juno promised. "I'm sure she's having a blast playing tag with her two new friends."

"Look!" Athena whispered, pointing up into the center of the room. Floating in the center of all the warehouse's hustle and bustle was a small, egg-shaped pod. Inside the pod . . . was Empress Geela. She stood tall and imposing, drifting over everything inside her protective bubble. Her awful pet, Tibbitt, was perched on her arm.

The girls hid behind some ductwork, hidden just outside Geela's line of sight. "Professor!" Geela cried out. Her voice echoed around the entire facility, amplified by some sort of sound system that ensured everyone would hear her while she inspected the goings-on from inside her floating chamber. "Show me my newest invention!"

Chamberlin scurried under a large pipe and covered his head with his hands. The five princesses, however, craned their necks for a better view. "This must be the weapon Captain Hansome wants us to report back on!" Luna said, stating the obvious.

On the ground, a large alien in a lab coat pulled an enormous tarp off a huge piece of machinery. Emblazoned on the side of the machinery was FOG-O-NATOR.

Empress Geela pushed a button inside her pod, and

the floating chamber swooped in closer to the enormous machine. "With this weapon," she declared, her voice echoing even louder in the huge warehouse. "I will be able to shroud the planets of the Pentangle in a permanent fog. The sun will no longer rise and shine. The planets will be cloaked in gloomy, glorious darkness—all day long!"

Hera gasped. "That's terrible."

"We need to report back to Captain Hansome immediately," Luna whispered. "He and . . . the *Resistance* . . . have to destroy it before she has a chance to use it!"

"Are you serious?" Juno asked in a hushed whisper. "You think I came all this way—and got this close to one of Geela's weapons—just so we could turn back and quit before the fun part?"

"Aren't these black spy suits the fun part?" Luna asked.

Juno shook her head. "We're going to destroy it. The Fog-O-Nator is never leaving this warehouse."

"That goes against Captain Hansome's instructions," Chamberlin protested. "He specifically said you were to find out what kind of weapon she was building and report back so . . . the *Resistance* . . . can figure out how best to destroy it."

"By the time we report back," Athena said, "it may be too late. We need to destroy it *now*!"

Moments later, the girls and a very nervous Chamberlin climbed up a narrow ladder on the far end of the warehouse. "We just need to get up on this ductwork," Juno said, racing up the ladder effortlessly. "We'll have the perfect view of the weapon's moving parts from overhead."

"In case anyone cares," Chamberlin mumbled. "I have a fear of heights . . ."

Behind him, Rhea asked, "Is there anything you're *not* afraid of, Chamberlin?"

Chamberlin paused for a moment, considering. "Doughnuts," he said finally. "And tea." As he began to climb again, he said, "But wait . . . cold tea gives me the willies. And sometimes, doughnuts have sprinkles. There is always the chance a sprinkle could fall off and go in your eye and—well, I guess that's to say, perhaps I'm also afraid of doughnuts."

Once they had all reached the top of the ladder, the six of them scurried cautiously on all fours across the web of ducts. From overhead, they had the perfect view of the Fog-O-Nator. Now, to figure out how to destroy it—without being destroyed themselves.

Below them, the professor was explaining the inner workings of the Fog-O-Nator to Geela. "There is only one weak spot on this weapon," he explained.

"That is unacceptable!" Geela shrieked, her voice

ringing out from one side of the warehouse to the other. "I don't believe in weakness."

"Well, Your Greatness, we have done our best to make this weapon as strong as possible—but in order to finish it in the timeline you required, we were not able to perfect the input valve."

"Explain yourself in my language," Geela screamed. "I don't know what you're talking about. Don't make me feel foolish, professor!"

"Yes, Empress," the professor said, cowering under Geela's floating pod. "You see, there is a tube just here—" He pointed to a huge metal pipe that reached up toward the roof of the warehouse. "This tube sucks in air that is then converted to fog. If something were to fall inside this tube while the motor was running, well . . . " The professor broke off with a shrug.

"Well what?" Geela screeched.

"Well . . . the entire machine would be destroyed," the professor said with a meek smile. "It's a weakness, I admit. And for that I'm sorry."

The girls exchanged a look.

"Turn it on!" Geela ordered. "I want to see how it works."

"But Empress," began the professor. "We'll fill the entire warehouse with fog in a matter of seconds."

"Don't 'but Empress' me," Geela barked. "Turn it on."

"But—"

"No buts!" Geela pointed a long, perfectly manicured finger at the professor. "Do it!"

The professor flicked a switch and the Fog-O-Nator roared to life. "Just give it one minute to warm up," the professor said nervously. "Then you'll see what kind of power you will soon have."

"We need to move fast," Juno whispered urgently to the other girls. "You heard what that guy said—this place is going to be filled with fog in no time. We need to jam that tube and move on out."

"What are we going to jam it with?" Rhea asked.

Before they could figure it out, Geela's voice rang out over the loud speaker again. "Doughnut!" she blurted. "I want a doughnut while I wait for it to warm up."

A guard raced across the warehouse floor, a tray of doughnuts balanced precariously in his hands. As the girls watched, the guard tripped on a loose piece of machinery . . . and the tray of doughnuts flew up, up, up. They twisted and spun in the air, flying in dozens of different directions. "Chamberlin, watch out!" Athena cried as one of the doughnuts—a glazed one coated with rainbow sprinkles—raced straight toward him. The doughnut made contact with Chamberlin's leg, and the sprinkles scattered everywhere. One of them spun and twisted through the air, then hit Chamberlin in the eye.

With a delicate shriek, Chamberlin tumbled off the duct-work and dangled over the Fog-O-Nator.

Juno and Athena both lunged for him, grabbing his arms and pulling him toward safety. But it was too late—Geela had already spotted them. "Someone is in here! Destroy them!" she screamed, as fog began to fill the air.

"We need to go *now*," Rhea said as Geela's floating pod raced toward them. Several of Geela's Android army began to shoot at the girls. Because of the fog shrouding the warehouse floor, the shots all missed. Instead of hitting their intended targets, the blasters blasted a huge hole through the warehouse wall.

"My cardigan," Chamberlin said, tugging at his sweater sleeve as the girls pulled at his arms and legs. "It's stuck. I'm caught on something."

"Take it off," Athena ordered.

Chamberlin shrugged his arms out of the sweater. The girls pulled him the rest of the way up, leaving his sweater dangling from the ductwork by one loose piece of yarn.

"Let's go out through one of the holes in the side of the wall," Juno ordered. "We'll have to jump." She whistled, long and loud.

As the six spies raced toward a huge blaster hole in the outside wall, Athena snuck one last glance back at the Fog-O-Nator. "I can't believe we failed," she growled. "Because of a doughnut."

But then, something amazing happened. Empress Geela's floating pod whooshed into Chamberlin's sweater as she raced after the five princesses. The force of the impact knocked the sweater free. Gracefully, the hand-knit cardigan fell *down, down, down*—straight into the Fog-O-Nator's precious, delicate input tube.

With a mighty *glorph!* the machine belched and groaned. Sparks began to fly, and the whole thing burst into flames. Geela screamed. Fog swirled around the girls as they jumped out of the hole in the side of the warehouse and leaped toward the ground below.

"Ha *ha!*" Geela's voice rang out from inside the warehouse. "That is a sixty-foot drop. The intruders have all fallen to certain death."

But she couldn't have been more wrong.

Just before the five girls and Chamberlin hit the icy ground, they bounced off a squishy nest of purple fur that had been waiting to catch them. "Good girl," Juno said, patting Skitter's huge, inflated back. "Now, it's time to get back to the space bus. Our first rebel mission is *over!*"

CHAPTER 11

"I AM IMPRESSED BY YOUR RESULTS," CAPTAIN Hansome announced over the Resistance's secure holo-network later that day. The leader of the Resistance had explained to his new recruits that, because of the risk involved with in-person meetings, most of their interaction would be done via remote communication devices and holo-comms that would be provided by the Resistance. Luna was crushed to think that she couldn't flirt (and admire the captain's rippling shoulder muscles) in person more often. *"But!"* Captain Hansome went on. "I am also frustrated that you took such risks during your mission. You were specifically told to scout and report back—not to destroy the weapon yourselves. You could have been hurt or, worse, caught."

"But we weren't caught," Juno said defiantly.

"But you could have been," Hansome said, jutting out his chiseled chin.

"But we weren't," Juno repeated.

"But you *could* have been," Hansome said.

"It was basically an accident anyway," said Juno.

"Enough!" Athena said, cutting them both off. "There is no sense arguing about it now. The deed is done. We snuck in, we performed our mission, and we also ended up performing *your* mission. All in all, it should be considered a success for the Resistance."

". . . the *Resistance!*" Hansome echoed. Then he shook his head, as if to clear it, and went on. "I must admit that I underestimated the five of you."

"And Chamberlin," Hera said sweetly. "If it hadn't been for Chamberlin and his sweater, the Fog-O-Nator would be churning out yucky-blucky fog all over the Pentangle Galaxy right at this very moment."

Chamberlin smiled modestly. "I am proud to have served . . . the *Resistance*. It was my pleasure."

"Indeed," Hansome said. "Thank you to Chamberlin as well. Now, we need to figure out what your next mission should be."

"Next mission?!" Chamberlin blurted out, choking on a sip of tea. "There will be no *next* mission!"

Hansome laughed. Luna quickly joined him. "Of course there will be another mission," Hansome said, chuckling.

"Silly Chamberlin," Luna added.

Hansome became serious again and said, "I will consider what your next task shall be and get in touch with you again shortly. In the meantime, you should prepare for the challenges that lie ahead. Hansome . . . *out!*" The holo-screen fizzled and went black.

"He's gone!" Luna shrieked. She dove for the holo-screen, staring into the blank void where Hansome's face had been just a moment before. "I miss him so much already."

"I'm sure he misses you, too, Snookie-kins," Rhea said in a sappy voice.

Luna glared at her. "He and I have a connection," she said, pouting.

"What do you think Hansome meant when he said 'prepare for the challenges that lie ahead'?" Athena asked.

"Fight training," Juno said. "Survival skills. If any of you actually came face to face with Geela or her Android army, it wouldn't be pretty. Sheer luck is the only thing that got us out of that warehouse last night. And me and Skitter."

"Don't give yourself all the credit," Luna snapped, still pouting.

"Oh, come on," Juno said, rolling her eyes. "If I hadn't been there to take the lead, you would all still be standing around trying to figure out how to *get* to the Ice Desert. You're all a bunch of princesses with absolutely no instincts for survival, reconnaissance, or spying."

"Juno is not wrong," Chamberlin said quietly. "None of you is equipped for this kind of work. If you are going to continue to perform rebel missions, I insist that you all learn to take better care of yourselves."

"I take great care of myself!" Luna protested. "I keep my skin hydrated with custom-blended moisturizers, I have regular facials, I get exfoliating salt scrubs twice monthly, my weekly mani-pedis—"

Chamberlin cut her off. "That is not the kind of care I am talking about. I'm talking about self-sufficiency and independence. You don't even know how to make your own bed!" he snapped. "I also know for a fact that none of you knows how to boil a kettle of water, you are incapable of cleaning up after yourselves, and one of you has been so spoiled by your servants that you have forgotten to flush the toilet *countless* times since our escape. Just imagine what would happen if you were in a situation where you *had* to take care of yourself in order to survive. It would be a disaster."

"On Junoia, there is a custom that when royals turn ten, they are sent into the wilderness to survive on their own for a month," Juno told the others. "I can't make my own bed—and, frankly, don't want to learn—but I do know how to protect myself in dangerous situations."

"Your parents sent their ten-year-old out into the wilderness for a month *alone*?" Hera asked, obviously horrified. "Who tucked you in at night? Who read you your bedtime story?"

"Who prepared your meals?" Luna asked.

"Where did you go to the bathroom?" Rhea wondered aloud.

"Things are different on Junoia," Juno said with a shrug. "My family believes it is essential that a young woman learn how to take care of herself in challenging situations. I would be happy to teach you all to fight, if you'd like me to."

"No thanks," Luna said in a bored voice. "I don't want to chip a nail. I have a feeling we might not get to a manicurist anytime soon . . ."

"A broken nail will be the least of your worries if you have to face-off against Geela," Athena chided her. "Juno, teach us everything you know."

★ ★ ★ ★ ★

"Ohhhhh," Rhea moaned, curling into a ball on her bed. "This must be what it feels like to be chewed up and then spit out by a krag. I'm so sore!"

"I think I might be dying," Luna whimpered. "Someone get me a juice!"

Hera, whose body was twisted into a complicated yoga pose on the floor, muttered, "Breathe happiness in, push the anger back out . . ."

Athena inspected her knuckles, which were bruised and cracking. "How long do bruises last?" she asked aloud. "Will my hands be scarred like this forever?"

"Oh my Grock!" Juno growled. "We haven't even gotten to hand-to-hand combat! All you've done is throw a few punches at poor Rand, who is probably a whole lot sorer than any of you. This is the easy stuff."

"Easy?" Luna yelped. "My muscles are so tired that I don't think I'll ever be able to get out of bed again. How are we supposed to go out on stage tomorrow for the outdoor music festival we're supposed to be performing at? I might need to be rolled out in a wheelchair."

"Get up and quit complaining," Juno ordered. "Do you want to be ready for our next mission, or not?"

"Aren't there other ways we could prepare?" Rhea asked. Suddenly, she brightened. "Ooh, I know what I can do. I'm going to add a little flare to our rebel outfits. I think I'll add a hint of color so we don't look like a giant blob of black when we're on our missions."

"Yeah," Juno muttered. "Looking good is just as important as learning to stay alive."

"Great!" Luna said. "If looking good is important, then I'm going to take a nap. If we want me to look my best for tomorrow's show, I am in serious need of beauty sleep."

While Luna dozed and Rhea figured out a way to jazz up their rebel outfits, Athena embarked on a project of her own. "What are you doing?" Juno asked, plunking down on Athena's bed. Athena had collected up all the small electronics, makeup, and fashion accessories they had on board the space bus, and was now expertly breaking them all open. Tiny screws, batteries, wires, and lipstick caps littered the top of her bed. Athena was hunched over everything, fiddling with a bunch of wires.

"I realized on our last mission that if we had gotten separated, there would have been no way for us to reconnect out there in the Ice Desert. Without communicators, we are putting ourselves in danger. So I'm trying to make us new devices that will help us during our missions."

"You're trying to *make* communicators?" Juno asked, furrowing her eyebrows. "Do you have any idea how to do that?"

"Yes," Athena said simply. "You were given survival training as part of your royal education. I, on the other hand, was enrolled in engineering courses. One could argue that engineering is far more useful as a life skill. I am using what I learned to try to fashion some home-made spy tools."

Juno nodded and settled in across from her. "That's not a bad idea."

"Thank you," Athena said, giving her a small smile. "We all have things that make us useful to the group."

"Even Luna?" Juno joked.

"Yes," Athena said seriously. "Even Luna." Athena slipped a giant moonstone ring onto Juno's finger. Then she opened up a tube of lipstick and held it up in front of her own mouth, preparing to speak into it. "These are both intended to be communication devices for us to use on our missions. Let's see if they work, shall we?"

"I have no doubt they'll work perfectly," Juno said with a sly grin. She hopped off the bed and stepped outside the girls' room. She lifted the ring to her mouth and spoke into it softly, "From what I can tell, you don't fail often, Athena. That's what makes us such a good team."

CHAPTER 12

"CALLING ATHENA," HERA YELLED INTO A SMALL compact mirror after lunch the next day. "Are you there, Athena? Come in, Athena!"

"Yes, Hera," came Athena's rather irritated reply a moment later. "I hear you, loud and clear. The communicators all seem to be working, so perhaps you should focus on getting yourself ready for our gig? Also, you don't need to *yell* into the devices. You can speak into them in an ordinary voice and we'll be able to hear you."

"Right!" Hera yelled. She stepped into the bedroom with the other girls and slipped the mirrored compact communicator into the pocket of her spy suit. The compact was one of six communication devices Athena had built. She had also turned a tube of lipstick, a moon-stone ring, an enormous jeweled pendant, a nonfunc-tioning graphic design e-pen that Juno had found on Borana, and Rhea's old-school watch into communica-tors. Whenever she had a few minutes (between band practice, songwriting sessions, and fight training with Juno), she spent them tinkering around, trying to assem-ble more devices—extending ropes and hooks, undetect-able recording devices, spy glasses, portable tracking devices—that might help them on future missions. "These little talky things are so much fun to play with! I can't wait to try them out on our next mission for . . . the *Resistance*."

"They're not toys," Athena snapped. "They're tools. Part of our spy weaponry."

"That doesn't mean they can't be fun," Rhea pointed out.

"Know what's even more fun?" Luna asked without turning away from the quick-moving wall of images that was splashed across the wall of the girls' bedroom. She beamed, flicking through image after image of her-self on stage. "We're turning up in a lot more searches lately. It's not just Bradbury's fan site—when I search on Luna and the SPACEPOP, it turns up three hundred forty-three hits!"

Since their impromptu park concert on Heralda,

SPACEPOP had been getting a lot more attention. Chamberlin had reluctantly broken down and gotten the girls an old computer (with horrifyingly basic 2D images and super unsophisticated voice and print recognition technology), so now Luna spent most of her waking hours searching galactic entertainment sites, digging for any mention of herself . . . and sometimes the rest of the band.

Now that the band had a way to interact with the outside world, Luna had also started replying to comment threads and blog posts that mentioned the band, in order to develop a rapport with their growing fan base. She was the only one of SPACEPOP who had made time to interact with fans, and the other girls all appreciated her taking the lead on their fan chats. She had started to develop a SPACEPOP website, too, which was very heavy on Luna images—but at least they now had an online presence. "Someone on this site said my voice sounds like spun Heralda honey. That's a compliment, right?"

"Have you tried searching the name SPACEPOP *without* including Luna in the search, too?" Juno asked. "You might dig up even more hits."

"SPACEPOP wouldn't be SPACEPOP without me," Luna said seriously. She turned away from the wall of moving galactic web images and smiled brightly at her own reflection in the mirror. "You look gorgeous," she cooed to herself. She coated her lips in bright red lipstick and frowned. "Even if this color is *meteor* red instead of *meteoric* red. It's just not the same . . ."

As another little treat for the girls—after their first few successful shows—Chamberlin had begrudgingly ordered the girls some makeup and a few additional things they needed to complete their SPACEPOP wardrobe. He had let them each request two special things. Of course, each girl had given him a page full of "needs," begging him to splurge a little. But Chamberlin had wisely pointed out that if they got too many intergalactic deliveries, they would attract unwanted attention from the wrong sort of people. So each princess had to do without many of the things on her wish list. Luna's lipstick order had gotten slightly mixed up, and she was struggling to get over it.

The bus came to a stop on the ground, and Juno peered out the window. "We're here. Looks like the festival is really crowded. This is going to be another great chance to help build up our fan base."

"Let's get out there and give the people of Rhealo what they're waiting for—me, of course!" Luna chirped. She raced out of the bus, waving as she sauntered through the crowds that were gathered on Rhea's home planet for a huge outdoor festival.

This show was an important one for SPACEPOP. They were one of the smaller acts in a huge outdoor concert weekend that had originally been scheduled to take place in an amphitheater near the Rhealo capitol. The Rocket Boys were the headline act, and they were well known throughout the galaxy for drawing an enormous crowd. SPACEPOP was hoping to introduce its music to some of the Rocket Boys fans.

But when Geela had found out about the festival, she had ordered the organizers to feature *her* as the headline act . . . or cancel it. The lead organizer of the show had refused to invite Geela to perform, so she had him imprisoned and then blew up the amphitheater. As an act of rebellion, a group of music lovers had arranged for the show to go on at a remote landing strip outside the capitol. There were multiple stages set up, and different bands were assigned to different stages—bigger, more prominent stages with ample shade for the well-known acts; smaller, more remote stages for the less-famous bands—throughout the afternoon.

"I'll check in with the people in charge," Athena offered. "We need to find out what stage we're playing on." She weaved through the crowds, returning a few minutes later with bad news. "We're on stage five . . . of five."

"Is five the best one?" Luna asked, looking excitedly at the main stage. It was enormous, floating and spinning in the center of everything.

Rand appeared behind them then, lugging a huge speaker. "Stage five is the one by the toilets," he announced. "Way over there." He pointed off into the distance— beyond the crowds, past the food stands, and miles away from the energy of the main stage. There was a puny brown stage squeezed into the open space just beside the portable toilets. Another band—one none of them had ever seen or heard of before—was playing to a nonexistent crowd. There was one lone person, who looked like she was lost or waiting for a toilet to be free, standing near the stage.

"Do they have any idea who we are?" Luna griped. "We are *way* too big a deal to be playing on the loser stage. I refuse."

"You can't refuse," Athena said diplomatically. "This is how bands start. You build slowly and earn your fans. Next time we play a festival with a bunch of bands that are better known than we are, we might get upgraded to the second worst stage. Then the middle stage, and we'll eventually be the lead act. It will happen. We just have to give it time."

"No," Luna pouted. "This is absolutely humiliating. I'll play at small clubs and even sing for tiny audiences where at least we're the main act, but there's no way I'm pretending to be happy in front of a crowd of zero on the worst of five stages. It's going to stink over there, and the stage doesn't even have lights! I'm too good for this." She stomped off in the direction of the space bus.

Rand looked to the other girls, trying to figure out what to do with the gear he had strapped to his back. "Should I bring everything back to the bus?" he asked sadly. "Are we leaving?"

"Nope. Load up the stage, Rand," Rhea said, shrugging at the rest of the band as she made a split-second decision. "We've got to go on, with or without our lead singer."

As soon as Rand had wandered off to get everything set up, Juno grumbled, "She's such a diva. We're better off without her."

"We don't need a lead singer with an ego—or hair—as big as Luna's," Rhea agreed.

"She's acting like a child," Athena snapped.

"She's just feeling disappointed," Hera said, trying to defend her. "Luna isn't used to not getting her way—none of us are, really. Her ego is bruised."

"Our reputation is going to be more bruised than her ego if we have to go on without a singer," Rhea said. "It's completely selfish of her to bail on us."

"I'll talk to her," Hera said calmly. "Let me see if I can get her to change her mind."

"We don't need her," Juno insisted.

"That's not true and you know it," Hera said rationally. "We *do* need her—and I think when we remind her of how much the galaxy needs us and our music, she'll come around. Let me try to mend things." Without waiting for anyone to disagree with her again, Hera skipped toward the space bus.

"Luna?" she said quietly, stepping into Luna's sleeping pod.

"What?" Luna snapped, her head buried under her pillow.

"Can you please come out and sing?" Hera asked softly. She placed Roxie and Adora on Luna's bed, urging them to tickle Luna out of hiding. Adora refused—she hated to annoy anyone—but Roxie was happy to tussle and tickle Luna until she broke down and smiled. Giggling, she peeked out from under the pillow. Hera smiled back at her. "Are you sure you want to give up this chance for more people to hear our music?"

Luna rolled her eyes, then began absentmindedly rubbing Adora's tummy. The little creature moaned and kicked one leg. "No one is going to hear us. We're playing to a bunch of toilets. There are literally *no* fans at the fifth stage. It's totally humiliating."

"Humiliating for whom?"

"For me!" Luna said. "This is such a waste of time."

"It's not a waste of time," Hera said calmly. "Luna, I think you're forgetting the point of this band. When Geela took over our planets, we were all ordered to hide away and wait for the trouble to pass. But we decided that we wanted to fight back, in the only way we could, right?"

"Yeah," Luna said. "By becoming famous rock stars. That's the only way we're going to make a real difference."

Hera shook her head. "We're not princesses anymore. We can't just snap our fingers and make things happen the way we used to. We need to build this thing slowly, from the ground up, and that means it will be a little harder and take a little longer than we're accustomed to."

"It just seems impossible," Luna huffed. "I hate seeing all the horrible things Geela has done to our planets and not be able to do something *now*. We've spent all this time practicing and writing songs so we can play to these tiny crowds . . . I'm sick of it."

"But tiny crowds are better than no crowds," Hera replied. "If you just sit here in the bus, sulking, there's absolutely *no* chance of anyone hearing you. If you go out there, and you give it your all, there's a chance *someone* might hear you." She paused, then added excitedly, "Bradbury is the perfect example. That first show we played at Air Bar—well, it seemed awful, right? But if we had skipped it because the crowd looked absolutely dead, we never would have met Bradbury. And if we hadn't met Bradbury, then we wouldn't have had any fans at the show on Heralda. Little by little, we're getting our message across."

Luna nodded slightly.

Encouraged, Hera went on, "If we hadn't played that show on Heralda, we wouldn't have caught Captain Hansome's attention and been recruited for . . . *the Resistance*." She grinned at Luna. "Each show has its purpose—just like each of *us* has our purpose in the band. We need you, Luna. Don't let us down."

Luna sighed. "You're right." She sat up and gave her a hug. "I'm sorry I stormed off." Quietly, she added, "I know I can be sort of stubborn sometimes—and maybe I'm a little hard to deal with every once in a while—but it's just that I'm afraid of this new life, you know? I'm scared, Hera. Geela is so cruel, and she's done so much so quickly."

Hera nodded. "That's why we can't give up. We need to get our old lives back—but we can't do that if we just camp out in this space bus and sulk."

Luna smiled slightly. "Yeah, you're right again."

Roxie chittered and launched herself into the middle of their hug. "She's trying to tell you I'm *always* right," Hera giggled. "Now, come on. Fix up your lipstick, and let's get out there and entertain every single person who comes over to use the bathroom! We'll show them SPACEPOP deserves the main stage from now on!"

As it turned out, *plenty* of fans came out to hear SPACEPOP. Although their stage wasn't flashy or centrally located (and there was a distinctly unpleasant odor in the vicinity), SPACEPOP had already started to build enough of a fan base that there was a medium-size smattering of fans who had come specifically to hear them play. The five princesses' pets also scurried around the festival grounds, urging concertgoers to make their way out to stage five to hear the girls' set. By the end of their show, a respectable crowd had gathered to cheer for them and sing along to "We 'Bout to Start Something Big."

"I'm glad you begged me to come back," Luna said to Hera as the girls boarded the space bus later that day. "That was a pretty good show. The portable toilets might have actually improved the acoustics."

"You sounded wonderful, girls," Chamberlin said, greeting them at the door of the bus. "Now, please—hurry inside. We just received a communication blast, and it says it's time sensitive."

"Is it from Captain Hansome?" Luna asked brightly, hustling through the door.

"Just have a listen," Chamberlin said. "It's a self-destructing pod and has pesky security measures encrypted in the device, so I didn't get to listen to his message before you returned."

The girls all gathered around a tiny message pod. The small sphere glowed orange and green, and when they pressed each of their fingertips to the outside of the pod for security verification, Captain Hansome's voice rang out as clear as a bell. "Good afternoon, rebels," he said.

"Good afternoon, Captain," Luna whispered back.

Rhea nudged her. "He can't hear you—it's a recording."

"Yeah, I *know*," Luna snapped back. "I'm just being polite."

"My sources tell me you are on Rhealo," the recording went on. "I have your second mission, and hope that this time you will be better at following orders. We need you to sneak into the transport bays on the eastern edge of Rhealo's capital. Once inside, please put tracking devices on Geela's space-tankers so we will be able to track them to their next destination."

"Where are we supposed to get tracking devices?" Juno wondered aloud.

Hansome's voice said, "My special ops team hid one hundred tracking devices and some additional instructions inside Juno's bass drum after your show today. Rand will be delivering them to the space bus at any moment. One hundred trackers should be more than enough to get the job done."

Just then, Rand stumbled into the space bus and collapsed under the weight of Juno's drum kit. He yelled out, "Not to complain, since it's my job to haul this stuff, but this drum kit is *heavy* today," he gasped, panting.

"Sorry, Rand," Juno called out as Rand stepped back outside to gather up his next load.

"Good luck on your second mission," Captain Hansome finished. "You must complete the job before midnight, when Geela's army will be moving out. So make haste!" There was a short pause, then Hansome's voice said in a monotone, "This message will melt in ten seconds. Ten, nine, eight, seven, six, five, four, three, two, one . . ." As the girls looked on, the tiny pod melted into a puddle of messy goo on the space bus dash. Springle launched herself toward it and pressed several of her wiggly limbs into the mess. Then she ran around the room, leaving sticky marks all over everything.

"Lovely," Chamberlin sighed. "As usual, I'll clean up the mess. But how about this time, we consider *that* my contribution to the rebel mission, shall we? I'm staying home, where there will be a hot cup of tea and *no* angry guards."

CHAPTER 13

"ALL ABOARD!" RHEA CALLED OUT, WAVING THE other girls toward a bright blue air train in the center of Rhealo's capital city. She jumped into the train and held the door open, urging the others to hurry. "Pick up the pace, girls. The next express train doesn't come for an hour, and if we miss this one, we miss the mission."

Luna pinched her nose closed and stepped aboard. "Can you imagine what kind of *germs* are lurking inside this train?"

Rhea shrugged and readjusted the bag of trackers she had slung over her shoulder as the train whooshed out of the station. She gazed up at a huge poster hanging on the inside wall of the train. Each of the five princesses' faces were splashed across the poster, along with WANTED and REWARD scrawled across the bottom. These Wanted posters had been cropping up all over the galaxy. Geela was obviously eager to capture the five girls so she could consider her takeover a total success. Each of the girls felt a small glimmer of pride every time they stood under one of these and failed to be recognized.

As SPACEPOP changed into their spy gear after the show, Rhea had decided that the easiest way to get to the eastern edge of Rhealo's capital was to take public transportation. Their tour bus was far too conspicuous, she'd pointed out, and a blown-up Skitter would be impractical for getting them from one side of the city to the other without being seen. The space taxi companies had all been taken over by Geela's employees, which made them off limits. Thus, a bus or train was the only thing that could shuttle them to the city outskirts in a hurry.

One of the very few positive side effects of Geela's takeover was that air trains and space buses throughout the galaxy now all ran on time—mostly because people were too terrified to leave their homes unless they absolutely had to. There was never a backup in the traffic lanes since the usual hustle and bustle of people shopping and going to work and meeting up with friends had come to a standstill. So right at the scheduled time of 10:23—with their spy outfits covered with ridiculous capes and several of Chamberlin's cardigans—the girls boarded an express train to the eastern edge of the city.

Luna was *not* pleased about their mode of transport. And she made sure everyone knew it. "Are we there yet?" she whined, gazing out the train's dirty window at the stark, angular buildings that surrounded them. "*Now* are we there? Does anyone have any sanitizer?"

At the second to last stop, a cluster of Geela's guards boarded the train and stood just a few feet from the princesses. Rhea pulled her hood farther over her face, and the other girls followed suit. The four guards gave them a brief once-over, but didn't connect them to the five faces on the Wanted poster. "What are you doing out at this hour?" one of the guards snapped at them. "It's past curfew."

"We are on our way home," Rhea answered quietly. "We were at a Geela support rally in the center of the capital."

The guard grunted. "Very well." Then she turned away to chat with the other guards, apparently satisfied that they were sharing the train with Geela supporters.

When the train reached its final stop, the black-clad rebels waited until the group of guards had disembarked, then they stepped off the train. The girls hid in the shadows until the air train platform was clear, then peeled off their cardigans and capes and raced down the moving staircase to street level.

Cloaked in their black spy suits, the girls ran through the streets, making their way toward the enormous transport bays and open spaces beyond the warehouse district. According to the instructions Captain Hansome's team had hidden inside Juno's drum kit, Geela was currently storing all her space-tankers in the transport bays at the far outskirts of Rhealo's capital.

As they prepared, Rhea explained to the other girls that each of these bays spilled out onto wide open spaces used as landing pads by larger space vehicles—supply tankers, interplanetary passenger transports, military vessels, and the like. Since Geela had taken over the planet, only the empress's vehicles were allowed to use the landing pads and bays. All large shipments in to and out of Rhealo had been halted for the foreseeable future, and the only way to get from one planet to another was to charter a smaller transport with funds most Rhealo residents didn't have. This was yet another way Geela was choking the residents of the galaxy.

By the time the girls reached the transport bays, it was already ten minutes to twelve. Hansome had told them the empress's fleet of space-tankers switched locations at midnight every night to avoid an enemy attack. "We only have a few minutes. We'll need to split up if we're going to have any hope of getting trackers on all of the vessels," Athena said. "Let's meet up here afterward—this is our rendezvous point."

"We can use our communicators if we get lost!" Hera chirped, happily waving her compact in the air. She couldn't wait to use her spy gadgets on a real mission.

"Yes, Hera," Athena said. "If you got lost or needed help, that would be the perfect time to use your communicator."

Hera rubbed her hands together, excited. "Yippee. I can't wait!"

"Everyone ready?" Athena asked. "There are five transport bays. That means one for each of us. There are probably ten tankers parked in each bay, so we'll need to move fast!"

"And remember," Rhea said, glancing around. "*Don't get caught.*"

"Can I *please* just trash a couple of Geela's tankers? Pretty please?" Juno pleaded.

"No," Athena said, cutting Juno off. "Tracking the tankers to their next location will be of more use to the Resistance. Let's prove to Hansome we are capable of following instructions and execute at least *one* mission as requested. I have a feeling we will be rewarded with even better missions in the future."

"Fine," Juno snapped. Then she raced away, calling

over her shoulder, "I'll take bay five. Whoever places the most trackers before midnight wins. Go!"

Juno dashed away from the other girls, racing toward the farthest bay at a full-out sprint. She felt confident she could place a tracker on every single one of the space-tankers in her bay and be back at the rendezvous point before any of the other girls had finished their piece of the mission.

All five girls had studied the tracking devices before they set off on the mission and discovered they were very elementary—small, thin, clear rubberlike discs with an adhesive on one side. To use them, you simply peeled away the backing and stuck them to the thing you wanted to track . . . like a giant bandage. Since they were flexible, they were supposed to mold to the shape of the object and blend in.

Juno hid under the hulking mass of one of the space-tankers. Then she dug into her bag and pulled out her first tracker. She glanced around, making sure no one could see her in the dark recesses at the back of the bay. She peeled off the backing, pressed the tracker to the space-tanker's hull, and stepped back.

Plop.

Juno scowled. The tracking device had popped off the ship and splatted to the floor. Juno's heart pounded, her nerves on edge. She glanced around again, then hastily reached down to the floor and scooped up the tracking device. She pressed it to the ship again, holding it in place for a few extra seconds to get the adhesive to stick.

Plop.

Again, it fell to the floor. She dug in her bag, fumbling around for another tracker. "Come on," she begged. "Let this one work." But when she peeled off the backing, she found the second tracker wouldn't hold either. She growled as she tried a third. No luck. Clearly, she was going to have to come up with plan B.

Taking a deep breath, Juno slipped along the back wall of the bay to the other side of the building. She got down on all fours and scuttled toward a mechanic's truck. When she was sure no one was watching, she scrambled up onto the truck and fumbled around in a pile of stuff until she found a tube of something she *knew* would work: Moon Glue.

With a proud smirk, she pulled off the cap with her teeth, squeezed a glop of glue on the back of a tracker, and pressed it onto one of the space-tankers. It stuck!

"One down," she muttered. "Nine to go . . ."

In bay four, Rhea was having the same issue.

"Captain Hansome looks good," she muttered, as she fumbled with the adhesive on a tracker, "but I sometimes wonder if that guy's working with a full deck."

Like Juno, Rhea had also come up with a creative

solution for attaching her trackers: hat pins. She always had some on hand, just in case her own hat came loose during a show or someone needed a wardrobe adjustment. She dug deep and unearthed a small pile of the sharp, pointed, pearl-encrusted pins. Then she jabbed one through a tracker and pressed the pin into the spacetanker's aluminum hull.

She smiled at her handiwork. "That will do."

As usual, practical Athena had prepared for any possible issues that might arise. So when she discovered the tracking devices were equipped with faulty adhesive, she reached into her bag and grabbed the double-sided tape she had brought along for just this reason.

"Athena," Hera hissed into her communicator. "Come in, Athena!"

"Yes, Hera?" Athena replied in a clipped voice, her breaths coming quickly.

"My trackers won't stick!" Hera was close to tears. When she arrived at bay two and found that the tracker wouldn't stick, she had optimistically tried every single one of the devices in her bag, maintaining hope that the next one she tried might work.

Athena's answer came back immediately. "Use something else to stick them on."

Hera began to say, "But what?" then stopped herself. She knew the other girls thought she was naïve and a little foolish and needed extra care sometimes. Hera didn't usually worry too much about what others thought of her, but she did long for the other girls to respect her more. If she could come up with her own solution to the problem, perhaps she could earn their respect. "Okay, thanks, Athena. Over and out."

Hera closed her eyes, methodically removing everything but the problem at hand from her consciousness. She transported herself to her happy place—a field full of moonberries near her family's castle. The sweet smell of the fresh fruit made Hera feel inspired and calm.

In fact, she had begun to carry around a pack of moonberry gum so that whenever she needed a little pick-me-up . . . "That's it!" Hera whispered, her eyes snapping open. "Gum! Gum is sticky!"

She dug into her pocket, popped a piece of moonberry-flavored goodness into her mouth, and began to chew.

In bay one, Luna was feeling smug and completely satisfied. *Spritz!* At one minute to midnight, just as the fleet of space-tankers fired up their engines, Luna squirted one final spritz of her "defy-gravity" hair serum onto the back of her last tracking device, pressed it onto the hull of a space-tanker, and grinned. The sticky hair spray worked like a charm.

As the first of the tankers rolled out of the bay and set off into the night, Luna spritzed her hair into place, then dashed toward the rendezvous spot. Her mission had been a complete success—all thanks to her hair.

A half hour later, the girls were on a train zooming back toward the center of the capital. They were buzzing with excitement and laughing about all the ways they had had to troubleshoot the faulty trackers. Between them, they had managed to tag every single one of Geela's space-tankers before they set off for their next spaceport.

"I think Captain Hansome should be pleased," Athena noted, reluctantly accepting a piece of Hera's moonberry gum to celebrate.

"Come on, girls," Rhea said. "We *rocked* that mission."

"Group hug?" Hera asked.

Juno and Athena shared a wary glance, then they both nodded. "Yeah," Juno said. "Today warrants a group hug, Hera." As they hugged, each of the girls thought about how far they had come in just a few weeks . . . but also how much more lay ahead for SPACEPOP and the Resistance in the coming months. Life in the Pentangle was still further from normal than ever, but at least it finally felt like the five princesses were doing *something* to help get their galaxy back on track.

PART FOUR: *MISSION CONTROL*

CHAPTER 14

"GET OUT OF THERE!" JUNO KICKED AT A SLEEK hologram of Geela in the middle of the living room. She leapt to her feet, her heart pounding. Juno had been trying to get a workout in, but Rhea and Hera were watching TV and it was completely distracting. Especially when they changed the channel and landed on *Geela's Rocky Remodel*. When Juno saw Geela's new renovation project, she had nearly lost it. For on this week's episode, instead of remodeling her *own* home, the empress was renovating Junoia's royal palace and broadcasting it for all of the Pentangle to see. "How *dare* she?" Juno growled, lunging for the hologram over and over again. "Get out of my house!"

Rhea flicked her wrist, making the hologram disappear. "Juno, it's just a hologram. You can't hurt her from here."

"You guys!" Luna came running into the living room, her cheeks flushed. "We just got a message from Bradbury."

"Another one?" Rhea asked, rolling her eyes. "How many times a day does that guy write to you?"

"Thirty or forty," Luna said with a shrug. "I'm keeping our fan base engaged. Oh, and I pretend I'm you girls in some of the messages—I hope you don't mind." Before anyone could answer, Luna went on. "But anyway, Bradbury just invited us to play at his uncle's wedding on Junoia! The band they had originally booked bailed at the last minute—they couldn't get off their planet because of some sort of travel restriction or something—so he asked if we could make it." She turned to Chamberlin and asked, "Can you get us to Junoia in a hurry?"

Chamberlin nodded. "We aren't far from there now. We could be there in a matter of a few hours." He drummed his fingertips together and whispered, "I do love weddings."

"I'll tell him we'll do it!" Luna said breathlessly.

"A wedding?" Juno asked, her eyebrows lifted. "Seriously? We're wedding singers now?"

"It's a *huge* wedding," Luna told her. "There will be five hundred people there, and some of them are *important*."

She poked at one of the images, and a brand new video of Bradbury began to play. He had uploaded a video to the message boards on the SPACEPOP fan homepage a few minutes earlier. In the video message, big, fat tears rolled down Bradbury's cheeks as he spoke into the camera. "I love you so so so so much," he said earnestly to the camera. "You're all so inspiring and . . . and . . . *I just want to be you!*" He rubbed his face, composing himself just enough to whisper, "I promise all the SPACEPOP fans out there that I will find out absolutely everything there is to know about our favorite band and report it back to you. Consider it my sacred duty." Bradbury sobbed again, and the screen went black.

Luna clapped. "Oh my Grock, he *loves* us! We made someone *cry!*"

"Is that a good thing?" Hera asked.

Luna nodded vigorously. "I've missed having crazy fans," she said. "Princess Lunaria de Longoria was worshipped and adored. And now, my alter ego Luna, SPACEPOP's lead singer, is worshipped and adored, too." She sighed.

Athena frowned. "Don't you think we should worry about this video? Just a bit?"

"Bradbury vowed to find out everything there is to know about us," Rhea added. "We don't want *anyone* to know everything about us. That's the whole point of being in disguise—we're keeping secrets."

Luna brushed her off. "Bradbury's harmless." She bounced away from the computer and began her pre-show makeup and hair routine. "Besides, he booked us a great gig—we should be grateful. Stop being such worriers."

As soon as the SPACEPOP tour bus set down on Junoia, Bradbury knocked on their door. "I'm so glad you could come," he said, breathless. In a sing-song voice, he added, "This is going to be a-*ma*-zing!"

He led them into the wedding venue—a beautiful stone garden, filled with waterfalls and small bonsai trees that seemed to glow from within. Bradbury ushered them past crowds of caterers, florists, and waiters. "You can get ready in here," he said, opening a door to reveal a sheltered changing area. "I didn't want to freak you guys out or anything by telling you this before you arrived, but . . . my uncle is actually a concert promoter here on Junoia. If you do a good job today, there's a really good chance you'll get some new bookings." He crossed his fingers and wiggled them in the air. "Fingers—and toes!—crossed."

Juno crossed her own fingers and managed a thin smile. "Fingers crossed." She patted him on the shoulder, then made her way into the dressing room.

Bradbury blushed, avoiding Juno's gaze. Rhea couldn't keep herself from laughing—it was obvious to everyone that Bradbury had a major crush on Juno. But it was just as obvious that she terrified him more than a little bit.

"Hey, Bradbury," Juno said from inside the changing room. She held up a big pile of fur. "What's with all the fur in here?"

"Fur?!" Hera screeched. "The poor animals!"

"It's not real fur," Bradbury assured her. "No creatures were harmed while making your costumes."

"I'm sorry—" Athena said, her face stony. "Our *what*?"

"Your costumes," Bradbury said, more loudly. "My uncle and his fiancée—his wife now, I guess!—are huge animal lovers." He looked at Luna, obviously confused. "In my messages, I explained that everyone at the wedding was asked to dress as his or her favorite animal—extinct or otherwise. We got five costumes ready for you—an otter, a fox, a cat, a chimp, and a narwhal. It's all they had left at the costume supply shop."

Luna glared at him. In a steely voice, she said, "You want us to dress . . . as animals?"

"I told you that in my messages," Bradbury said, his

voice strained. "And if you don't play, my uncle won't see how amazing you are, and the gig with the Vorks tomorrow night won't happen, and—"

"Luna?" Athena said, cutting him off. "Did you read Bradbury's whole message?"

Luna grinned sheepishly. "Not exactly. He sends a *lot* of messages." She turned to Bradbury. "*What* gig with the Vorks, Bradbury?"

"*Wellllll,*" Bradbury said. "You know the Vorks, right?"

"As in, the number one band in the galaxy?" Rhea asked. "Yeah, we've heard of them."

"*Wellllll,*" Bradbury said again. "Vindee, their lead singer, really likes your sound. She told my uncle to check you guys out, and if he likes you, too—well, he was going to book you as the opening act for the Vorks tomorrow night at the Junoia coliseum. It's a sold-out show—forty-five thousand fans!"

"Are you serious?" Luna shrieked.

"Totally," Bradbury said. "But the catch is, you have to impress my uncle first. And to impress my uncle, you're going to have to slip into these animal suits and sing your hearts out at the reception tonight."

Luna grabbed the cute cat costume before anyone else had a chance. "Dibs!" she yelled. "Let's do this thing, girls. We're going to open for the Vorks!"

Despite the band's bizarre costumes, the SPACEPOP

performance at Bradbury's uncle's wedding went really well. The best part of the night, though, was when Bradbury's uncle announced to the entire wedding party that SPACEPOP *would* be opening for the Vorks the next night at Junoia's coliseum. The girls all threw off their animal heads and cheered, then played "We 'Bout to Start Something Big" for a very excited crowd. They kept things hopping until well after midnight. By the time they got back to the tour bus, each of the girls was ready to curl up into a ball and hibernate.

But before their heads could hit their pillows, Chamberlin rushed into their room. "Your Highnesses, Captain Hansome is waiting to speak with you."

"Congratulations on booking your first major arena show," Captain Hansome said when the girls had gathered around the screen. "I have more good news for you."

"You're coming to visit?" Luna asked in an unnaturally high voice. She flipped her hair over her shoulder and beamed at the captain's hologram.

"Uh, no . . ." Hansome said. "But! The *Resistance* would like to request your help. This will be your biggest mission yet. I think you will enjoy it."

"We enjoy *all* your missions, Captain," Luna cooed.

Captain Hansome chuckled. "Wonderful. Now, as I was saying: your mission. While you are on Junoia, we would like you to track down the hidden server that houses and distributes all of Geela's television and radio broadcasts. We have information that this server is tucked away underground, in a carefully guarded bunker.

"We at . . . the *Resistance* want to shut down Geela's media circuits. If we can blast the server to smithereens, we will shut her down—for a while, at least—and take the opportunity to show *her* what it feels like to be silenced and controlled."

"Just like she's doing to the people of the galaxy!" Hera said, eyes wide.

The girls all nodded. Hansome was right: this was the mission they had been waiting for. It was time to shut Geela down.

CHAPTER FIFTEEN

TODAY WILL MAKE US OR BREAK US. OUR FIRST MAJOR CONCERT **AND** A REBEL MISSION . . . ALL IN THE NEXT TWELVE HOURS!

I'M ALREADY TIRED JUST THINKING ABOUT IT.

BE EXTRA CAREFUL TODAY, PRINCESSES. MAKE SURE THAT NO ONE RECOGNIZES YOU. DON'T LET THEM GET YOU.

WHO'S OUT TO "GET" THEM?

OH, UM, YOU KNOW . . . THOSE . . . CRAZY FANS! YEAH, HERE ON JUNOIA PEOPLE CAN GET PRETTY WILD SOMETIMES.

WE DON'T HAVE TIME TO COME BACK TO THE BUS AFTER THE SHOW. DOES EVERYONE HAVE WHAT THEY NEED FOR THE MISSION?

OH, THANK YOU, ADORA! I ALMOST FORGOT MY LIPSTICK COMMUNICATOR!

FROU-FROU OOH-LA-LA!

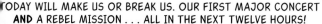

ARE YOU OKAY, JUNO?

I'M FINE. IT'S JUST A LITTLE STRANGE TO BE HOME.

SIGH!

SO MUCH HAS CHANGED SINCE I LEFT.

I WONDER IF MY LIFE WILL EVER GO BACK TO NORMAL . . .

SPACEPOP! I'VE BEEN LOOKING EVERYWHERE FOR YOU! I PAID EXTRA FOR AN ALL-ACCESS BACKSTAGE PASS!

BRADBURY!

COME ON! I CAN SHOW YOU TO THE DRESSING ROOM. I HAD ALL YOUR FAVORITE SNACKS DELIVERED, SO YOU WILL ALL FEEL VERY COMFORTABLE!

IT'S SWEET!

HOW DOES HE KNOW WHERE OUR DRESSING ROOM IS? AND WHAT OUR FAVORITE SNACKS ARE? IS IT JUST ME, OR IS THAT KIND OF WEIRD?

FINALLY, A DRESSING ROOM FIT FOR A PRINCESS.

I SUPPOSE THIS WILL DO . . .

THIS IS **MY** DRESSING ROOM. YOURS IS OVER THERE.

THIS? THIS ABSOLUTELY WILL NOT DO!

DON'T BE RIDICULOUS LUNA. THIS IS NORMA FOR A NEW BAND.

SPACEPOP! YOU'RE ON IN FIVE!

CHAPTER SIXTEEN

THE PRINCESSES OF THE PENTANGLE WERE READY TO GO FROM ROCK STARS TO REBELS!

THE SO-CALLED EMPRESS NOW CONTROLS ALL MEDIA IN THE PENTANGLE GALAXY. IT'S TIME FOR SPACEPOP TO SHOW GEELA WHAT IT FEELS LIKE TO BE SILENCED.

THEIR MISSION IS CLEAR: FIND GEELA'S HIDDEN SERVER . . . AND DESTROY IT!

ARE YOU SURE WE'RE GOING THE RIGHT WAY, JUNO?

JUST A HUNCH . . .

BUT I THINK THAT MIGHT BE GEELA'S HIDDEN SERVER.

EVERYONE, **STOP!**

ARE YOU OKAY?

DID YOU BREAK A NAIL?!

LOOK AT THE PRETTY EVENING BRAMBLE ROSE!

SERIOUSLY, HERA? IN CASE YOU'VE FORGOTTEN, WE'RE ON A REBEL MISSION. THERE'S DANGEROUS STUFF HAPPENING, RIGHT NOW.

EVERYONE, STOP AGAIN!

ENOUGH STOPPING TO SMELL THE ROSES—WE HAVE A JOB TO DO!

GEELA'S GUARDS!

WE NEED TO HIDE. EVERYONE, FOLLOW ME!

HAVE I MENTIONED THAT I DON'T ESPECIALLY ENJOY CREEPY TUNNELS?

OH, REALLY? I NEVER WOULD HAVE GUESSED.

THIS TUNNEL WILL LEAD US AROUND GEELA'S GUARDS AND BRING US CLOSER TO THE SERVER.

WILL IT ALSO GET US CLOSER TO A SHOWER? JUNOIA STINKS!

I THINK THAT'S THE EVENING BRAMBLE ROSE.

HOW ARE WE GOING TO GET INSIDE? THE GUARDS ARE BLOCKING EVERY ENTRANCE.

HAS ANYONE CONSIDERED THE FACT THAT SIX OF US MIGHT ATTRACT UNWANTED ATTENTION?

MAYBE WE SHOULD SPLIT UP TO FIND ANOTHER WAY IN. CHAMBERLIN, GO WITH JUNO AND LUNA.

HERA, RHEA— COME WITH ME.

FIND ANYTHING YET?

NOTHING YET . . .

UH-OH. LOOKS LIKE TROUBLE FOUND US!

189

190

TEN MINUTES LATER, HERA FOUND A DIFFERENT WAY IN . . .

I'M NOT USUALLY MUCH OF A PRINCESS, BUT THIS IS PRETTY GROSS—EVEN FOR ME.

. . . THROUGH THE GARBAGE CHUTE.

JUST A LITTLE FARTHER.

ONE WOMAN'S TRASH IS ANOTHER'S TREASURE. STALE DONUT, ANYONE?

I'M NOT SURE I WOULD GO QUITE SO FAR AS TO CALL THIS A TREASURE.

IT'S A WAY IN, ISN'T IT?

IS THAT GEELA?

THE EMPRESS OF EVIL IS HERE? CAPTAIN HANSOME DID NOT TELL US SHE WOULD BE HERE.

WE CAN'T LET HER SEE US. LET'S DESTROY THE SERVER, GET OUT OF HERE, AND CELEBRATE.

EASY PEASY.

SO . . . SHOULD I START SMASHING STUFF?

OR MAYBE I SHOULD TRY TO HACK INTO THE SYSTEM?

YOU KNOW HOW TO DO THAT?

I CAN PLAY GUITAR, SEW, HACK GIANT EVIL EMPRESS'S COMPUTERS— WHAT CAN'T I DO?

AHEM . . .

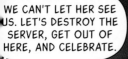

WE COULD ALSO TRY REVERSING THE CHARGE ON OUR COMMUNICATORS. I THINK I CAN TURN THEM INTO EXPLOSIVE DEVICES . . .

AHEM!

I COULD RUN OUT THERE AND GIVE HER A HUG. I SOMETIMES WONDER, IF GEELA HAD A LITTLE MORE LOVE IN HER LIFE, MIGHT SHE BE A LITTLE NICER?

AHEM!

SOMETHING CAUGHT IN YOUR THROAT AGAIN, CHAMBERLIN?

MUCH AS I LOVE ALL OF THOSE VERY DANGEROUS IDEAS, PERHAPS YOU COULD JUST . . . PRESS THAT BUTTON?

LET ME HANDLE THIS.

KABOOM!

INTRUDERS! DESTROY THEM!

CHAPTER 17

"WE DID IT!" SCREAMED ATHENA, PUMPING HER fist into the air. "Geela has officially been silenced!" The heat from the blast licked at her back as she and the other rebels raced away from the exploding server. The entire structure glowed orange, and the giant computer fizzed and popped.

Then horrible honking sounds began to echo out from somewhere inside the building. "Is that Geela *crying*?" Hera asked, looking back over her shoulder.

"Oh, no," Juno said. She grabbed Hera by the elbow and tugged her forward. "You're not feeling *bad* for her, are you?"

Hera jutted out her chin and continued to run. "Not

even a little bit. She destroyed our families' homes. She's holding our parents prisoner. Our planets are a mess. She's taken over our beautiful galaxy and encouraged the people—our people—to distance themselves from each other and fight among themselves. She deserves this . . . and much more."

Juno whacked her on the back. "Atta girl."

"You know who I *do* feel bad for?" Rhea asked as they ran toward the same space transport they had stolen from the guards earlier. They knew they had to get back to the relative safety of their space bus quickly, before Geela or her guards could catch them. There was no time to run all the way there. "I feel bad for all the people who invested weeks watching *The Empress*. With Geela's media networks down, they won't get to see the season finale tomorrow night. Who will she choose? We may never find out."

"I'm guessing she chooses *Geela*," Athena said blandly. "I don't see 'the empress' sharing her life with anyone other than herself."

As soon as the girls reached the transport, they all hopped in and clumsily pulled Chamberlin aboard. Their weary butler settled into the front passenger seat and began massaging his temples as the girls' collection of pets cuddled in around him. He closed his eyes and muttered, "I have shared just about enough of *my* life with the five of you. I suspect I may expire if there's much more of the kind of rigmarole we got into tonight."

"We have to find Luna," Athena said suddenly, while Rhea pushed at buttons to turn on the transport. Athena scanned the horizon. "I just hope she got Bradbury far away from the server building before that explosion, or we'll have more than a few questions to answer. I doubt our biggest fan is going to be a fan at all anymore if he realizes we're working for the Resistance. Bradbury is great, but he doesn't seem like the kind of guy who's going to love troublemakers."

Behind them, they could hear guards streaming out of the server building. Someone shouted, "Find the intruders! Destroy them!"

Juno took a deep breath. "Let's also hope Luna and Bradbury aren't *too* well hidden, since we have got to hit the sky—now."

"If you ask me, getting out of here about five minutes ago would have been preferable," Chamberlin muttered.

"No one asked you," Rhea said, grinning. She pushed the transport's throttle to full-speed and blasted across the rough terrain. Far off in the distance, behind a giant rock, something flashed. "There!" Athena said, pointing. "I think that was Bradbury's camera flash."

Rhea whipped the transport to the right, around some

jagged rocks, and squealed to a stop on the other side of the rock. Luna was singing to Bradbury, her voice loud and strained. "There you are!" Luna said, a panicked look in her eyes. "Are we all set? I think Bradbury has everything he needs now. We were just doing a nice, loud, private concert."

"Fun." Athena nodded. "Yes, we are all set here."

"Would you like a lift back to the coliseum, Bradbury?" Luna asked sweetly.

"With, uh . . ." Bradbury looked into the crowded transport, his eyes focusing on Juno. "With . . . all of you?"

"Hop in," Rhea said. "But I should warn you—I don't have my license."

"Oh!" Bradbury said, nodding solemnly as he squeezed into the crowded transport. "Is *that* what all of you were doing way out here? Helping Rhea practice for her spaceway exam?"

"Huh?" Rhea asked, giving him a funny look.

Hera giggled. "No, silly! We were out here to find G—"

Juno cut her off, trying to hide a smile. "Yeah, Bradbury. You're very perceptive. We were way out here so Rhea could practice her flying. You're *exactly* right."

Bradbury snapped a picture of Rhea behind the wheel of the stolen transport. "Can I post a picture of you practicing for your flying exam on my site? It makes you look really relatable!"

"Better not," Rhea said apologetically. The last thing they needed him to post was a picture of Rhea behind the wheel of one of Geela's guard's transports. Even if *Bradbury* didn't realize it was Geela's transport, surely *someone* would recognize what was happening if the picture were floating around online for the entire galaxy to see! "I don't want Chamberlin here to get in trouble for, uh . . ."

Chamberlin broke in, "For taking a group of unlicensed drivers out without helmets."

"What are you talking about? You don't need helmets to drive a space transport!" Bradbury laughed.

"Silly me," Chamberlin said. "I didn't realize times had changed so much since I was a young alien, learning to drive myself. I am rather old, you know. Many things about our galaxy have changed."

"Silly Chamberlin," Rhea echoed. She winked at him—grateful for his ridiculously believable cover, and even more grateful for Bradbury's foolishness—then threw the transport into gear. "Buckle up, everyone. It's time to fly."

Once they had dropped Bradbury back at the coliseum (with promises to give him the first-ever SPACEPOP exclusive interview soon) and the group was safely back inside their tour bus, the girls finally took the time to celebrate properly. There were hugs and high-fives all around, and Chamberlin pulled out a small tin of crater caviar and a package of Martian macaroons he had kept hidden for a special occasion. As they all filled up with goodies, Athena flicked on the holo-screen, and they all cheered some more . . . because the only image on any of the channels was a small, spinning G logo. No *The Empress*, no news, no Geela.

"Tell me everything!" begged Luna. "I can't believe I missed the end of the mission."

"I can't believe Bradbury showed up in the *middle* of a mission," Juno said, shaking her head. "Seriously, that guy is going to be bad for business."

"He's really sweet," Luna told her. "He does mean well—and he was very easily distracted. He also clearly hasn't figured out any of our secrets."

"Yet," added Athena. "Thank you for handling that situation, Luna. As it happens, your role was just as critical as the rest of ours in this mission. Bradbury could easily have foiled everything."

Luna smiled. "Thanks. And the best part is, I don't smell nearly as badly as the rest of you do. Come on, tell me everything—from the moment you left me, until you picked me and Bradbury up in the transport to come home."

"Home?" Rhea asked. She gestured around the tour bus, eyebrows lifted.

"For now," Luna said with a small smile. "It's the closest thing we have to home, isn't it? Now spill!"

The other girls were just about to launch into the story of their night when a tiny holo-ball blasted through the bus door. A moment later, a flickering, miniature Captain Hansome stood before them. "It appears things went well tonight?" he asked, flashing SPACEPOP a broad smile.

"It went very well. I took care of a *major* problem that came up and totally saved the day," Luna said, stepping in front of the other girls to pose in front of Hansome's hologram. She batted her eyes and said, "Mission accomplished, Captain."

"Tell me everything," Hansome said.

As soon as they got to the part about blowing up the server, Rhea announced, "Ka-boom! Now we don't have to watch or listen to Geela's ridiculous programming anymore. No more *Rocky Remodel*, *Cookin' with G*, or *The Empress*. She has been silenced."

"Well done, SPACEPOP," Captain Hansome said. "You have proven yourselves to be a worthy addition to our team. Tonight, thanks to you, we scored a major victory for . . . the *Resistance*."

"So that's it, then?" Chamberlin asked, cradling his tea in his hands. "We blew up the server and performed our final mission, so I assume you'll take over from here?"

"Ah, Chamberlin," Captain Hansome said, chuckling. "We have won *this* battle . . . but we are still in the midst of a war. Geela still has the royal families imprisoned in the Dungeon of Dark Doom, the five princesses of the Pentangle are on the run . . ." Here, the girls all shared a quick glance. Captain Hansome continued in a somber voice, ". . . and the citizens of our galaxy are more ill at ease than ever before. This battle is won—but the war is most certainly not over."

Chamberlin sighed. "I had a feeling you might say that."

"There will certainly be many more battles to fight," Captain Hansome said seriously. "Athena. Rhea. Hera. Juno. Luna. The time has come for you to decide: Are you ready for more?"

One by one, they each nodded. Chamberlin was ready for a rest, but his five royal charges were only getting started. The past few weeks had given them the opportunity to see what they were capable of. These five girls— who had gone from spoiled, pampered princesses to strong, powerful rebels in the space of just a few weeks— wanted nothing more than to take back their galaxy. They were ready to continue the fight. Athena spoke for the group when she said, "We're with . . . the *Resistance* all the way. Captain Hansome, we will do whatever it takes."

There was no doubt there would be many more battles to fight. But more importantly, there was also no doubt that the five princesses of pop were ready to *rock* the rebellion.

It was time to start something big.

ACKNOWLEDGMENTS

I AM INCREDIBLY GRATEFUL TO THE TEAM AT Genius Brands, who allowed me the opportunity to help develop this amazing brand. Thank you for trusting me to create a fun story with the characters and world!

Thanks also to the rock star crew at Imprint & Macmillan—Erin Stein, Nicole Otto, Natalie Sousa, Jennifer Gonzalez, Jennifer Edwards, Jill Freshney, Christine Ma, Raymond Colon, Ashley Woodfolk, and Molly Brouillette— for making this project so much fun.

A standing ovation to Jen Bartel for bringing these characters to life with your gorgeous illustrations.

Finally, thanks to Catherine Clark, Milla Downing, Ruby Downing, Henry Downing, Robin Wasserman, Michael Bourret, and Greg Downing—who all helped with plotting, kept me well fed and full of coffee, and are constantly helping me stay (somewhat) sane. You guys rock.

ERIN DOWNING can't sing or play the drums or keyboard . . . but after letting her guitar collect dust for years, she is *finally* learning to play it and hopes to someday open for SPACEPOP. Erin has written more than fifty books for young adults, tweens, and kids, including *Best Friends (Until Someone Better Comes Along)*, The Quirks, and the Puppy Pirates series (as Erin Soderberg), and the forthcoming novel *Moon Shadow*. Before becoming an author, Erin was a book editor and a cookie inventor, and also worked for Nickelodeon. She writes, watches TV, and eats out in Minneapolis with her husband, kids, and a very fluffy dog. More information about Erin's books can be found at erindowning.com.